HIGHLAND SANCTUARY

Published by Magic Wolf Publishing

Copyright © 2016 by Brina Cary
ISBN: 978-1-945409-05-9

Edited by Barbara Kirby

Cover Design and Interior Format

HIGHLAND SANCTUARY

THE MACDANIELS
BOOK ONE

BRINA CARY

ACKNOWLEDGMENTS

Thank you, Barbara Clark, for everything you do for me! You keep me on track with my writing, tell me when I'm procrastinating (which I do a lot), and edit my work into something amazing! My books are getting out into the real world because you work so hard and I adore you for it!

Thank you, Killion Group, for the wonderful cover! I'm so pleased that you were able to use the image that Stephanie Stone, of Stephanie Stone Photography, took for me, as a background! I absolutely adored those trees! I also love Jennifer Jakes' ability to turn my final work into this wonderful, professional book!

Thank you, Mom, for supporting me when I wasn't sure I could continue on. I've been so ill for a while now that there's been days that it's tough to get anything done. On those days, you magically appear and it makes my day!

Thank you to my nephews for making me smile, even when I'm up against deadlines and dealing with illness. You two are my world and I can't wait to see what you come up with next!

Thank you to my co-workers for cheering me on and being excited about my writing. Not once have they made me feel like it wasn't important. The confidence that gave me made me feel like I could do anything.

CHAPTER 1

POP! SUCH A LOUD SOUND. It echoed off the ranch style house, the tall pine trees that surrounded them, and the silent air around them. It slammed back into her with a force greater than anything she had ever known. Struggling to breathe, she watched as her brother's Boxer, Rocky, stood over him, growling menacingly. The protective gesture came too late for Finn though. The world was crashing down. Everything she loved… She couldn't move. What had once been a sanctuary for her was now a wretched, coldhearted, empty place.

Betrayal was thick in the air. It mingled with the scent of gun powder and blood. Her eyes were open wide, taking in every helpless moment as she stayed rooted to the spot where Matthew had pushed her. "No…" Her voice was hoarse, harsh with emotion. The paralysis began to wear off, slowly replaced with anger. Her breaths came in gasps, and tears threatened to fall. How dare he!

"Finn…," she whispered in anguish. His name slid from her lips as the tears that she had held back for so long slid down her cheeks. The only one to ever try to stop the pain she received at the bastard's hands, and he was dying—dying from trying to help her… Even from her spot she could see the blood that gurgled from his wounds. It was bright red with tinges of crimson — bright from oxygen. The bullet had hit his lungs. Helplessly, she watched as Finn coughed up blood… The last few breaths he would ever take had ceased, however, Rocky continued to try to protect him. Such a good dog.

Matthew grinned. The bastard grinned. As he turned the gun back to her bile rose in her throat. Stalking forwards, he put the gun behind his back and tucked it into the waistband of his jeans. "Jer, keep an eye on the dog."

"Can't I just shoot him too?" The scruffy looking man eyed Rocky with wariness. Slowly shifting from foot to foot, he took a deep breath. With a nervous glance he waited, the gun aimed at Rocky. Silently, she begged the dog to stay where he was, where he might be safe from Matthew's wrath.

"Nah, he won't leave Finn. Damn dog's been protecting him for far too long. For the life of me, can't tell you why I like that dog but I do. Maybe it's because he's loyal, unlike some people." He glared at her. "Just keep an eye on him." Matthew pushed the long sleeves of his thermal shirt up to his elbows, showing off the dragon tattoo that ran from his bicep down his arm to his wrist. It had been there for years now, the ink faded with age. Squatting down in front of her, he pushed his shaggy black hair out of his eyes. He'd let it grow— so different from how it had been in the Navy. He had changed too… Guess a dishonorable discharge will do that to you. "Now, sweetheart, you and I have some things to talk about."

She stayed where she was on the ground, where he had pushed her. The wet dew on the grass soaked through her jeans causing the chill to spread — the chill that had begun with the first POP of the gun — the same POP that cause her brother to lay a few feet away. The chill ran throughout her body, but despite this her heart seemed to beat faster. It felt like it was going to burst from her chest at any moment. Run! Run! Run! Her brain screamed it over and over again, but still she couldn't move. All these warnings her body was giving her, all the flares of 'save yourself', but she was frozen. Her muscles locked in place from fear. Conditioning from years of his abuse had taught her one thing: moving or trying to run would only get her killed.

"Matthew, please… Stop!" He jerked her up by her forearm and drug her back to the house. A shoe slid off her foot. The dew quickly soaked her sock. Her toes went numb from the cold, matching her fingers. Throwing her against the vinyl siding, he laughed. As he threw his hands against the house on each side of her head she flinched. "Please… Just leave…," she begged. Closing her eyes against the onslaught of fear, she waited for his response. Fear, it came so natural to her when it involved him. Silently, she began commanding herself not to recoil at his touch, praying that her body would listen. It would only make him angrier if she made a single movement. Movements that radiated fear always made things worse — always made him edgier, determined to prove something.

"Open your eyes." She did as he commanded, bringing a grin to his face. "Good to see you still know how to listen to some things." His dark onyx eyes burned into her hazel ones. "Your brother's as good as dead, Ames. He's not coming back. The idiot should never have intervened in the first place. It's just between you and me. You should know by now that I wouldn't tolerate anyone coming between us. I told you that after your… betrayal…"

The word "betrayal" was spat like it caused a bad taste in his mouth just to consider it. It also came out as hate, pure and simple hate. He had used that to justify so much of what he had done to her. She had been trying to save lives. Was Matthew so hung up on money that he couldn't see that? That he refused to see that? An anonymous tip, that's what she had left. Nothing to connect him to it. All in the name of saving lives… and it had cost her hers. So much pain. So many regrets. How was she to know that they would trace the tip back to her?

Now Finn was dead. There was no time, or way, to put things right. It was just her that was left, all because she wanted to save a child — random child no one else seemed to care about but her. Everyone seemed to be paying for her mistakes. Maybe she deserved what damage Matthew wrought. Maybe she deserved everything that was happening. Maybe he was right. Maybe she never should have betrayed him. If she hadn't though, another innocent child would be dead, having been used as a mule to transport drugs, and she would be to blame for that too. One child vs everyone she had ever loved? Was it worth it?

He tilted his head and leaned forward, centimeters away from her bare neck. Breath hot and moist danced along her skin. Goosebumps raised on her arms. Desire to flee clawed up from her stomach. Willing herself not to let her fear show, she tried to steel herself from the shaking that threatened to overtake her. As he took another deep breath on her neck, bile rose in her throat and her knees almost buckled. If only she could pass out, maybe death would come quickly. The hope was futile though. He wouldn't stand for it. He'd wake her just to kill her. "You smell so good. The things you do to me, even if you are just a whore."

"Please just let me go… You've taken everything from me! What more do you want!?!"

The sound of flesh hitting flesh hit her ears before she registered that he had slapped her. Stinging pain laced her cheek, however, the pain was her last concern. It was not like he had never hit her before. Heck, he had done a lot more than hit her. The scars that laced her skin were proof of that. "I told you to never raise your voice to me. Seems you have forgotten some of the rules after all, Ames." His hand was around her throat before she could even raise her arms to fend him off. "I think maybe I should just get this over with. Do you in once and for all. I really want to kill you. I just want to feel your pulse stop pulsing beneath my fingers and watch your eyes bulge. You know what it's like to die from asphyxiation?"

She felt his hand tighten slightly around her throat, the danger of the threat becoming more imminent. Was he that far gone? Looking in his eyes she knew. He was gone. Matthew was angry at her. Angry enough to finally kill her.

"You ruined everything, Ames. Cost me my job with the Navy. Now, you're costing me my livelihood." He leaned close enough for her to smell the whiskey on his breath. "Diego is gunning for me. If that shipment doesn't go down as planned then my head is on the chopping block. I've already lost one cozy set up because of you. I won't lose another. What did you tell them?"

Putting aside the fear that threatened to overwhelm her, she choked out, "Just… leave…."

His lips turned upward in a sick smile, a sinking feeling began in her stomach. "Oh, Ames. Tsk. Tsk. Tsk. You have forgotten. Such a shame. You were once so beautiful, so lovely. You used to know how to obey. Such a shame that you have forgotten. Guess I'll just have to remind you of the price." He squeezed tighter. She gasped for breath, but made no attempt to scream. The burning in her lungs told her that it wouldn't be long before she joined Finn. Then the nightmare would finally be over. She would finally be free. Matthew couldn't follow her to the afterlife, although he would probably try.

Distant sirens broke through the fog that had taken over. Was help coming?

The hand at her throat pressed harder. He meant business this time. "Amy, I swear. I swear that I'll kill you the next time I see you. Don't you dare tell anyone about this. I'll kill you if you say a single word."

Her brother was dead. Who would she tell? The only person that cared was lying a few feet away, his empty eyes staring at her. Cold and judging. Her brother was dead and the bastard was worried about who she would tell? More worried than he was about who she had already told.

"Do you understand?" When she failed to respond fast enough he pulled her forward away from the wall. A whoosh sounded in her ears as he slammed her back into it. "Do you understand?" Her lungs burned and spots danced in front of her eyes. At her nod he released her. The jelly that her legs had become refused to hold her as she fell to the ground gasping in breaths. "Good. See to it that you uphold your end, or it'll be the last thing you do."

It would be the last thing she did. He'd make sure of it. How could she possibly survive when there was no one left that would help? When no one was left that could help? How could she fight him when all of her strength had been stolen from her?

Had her strength really been stolen? Was she no longer who she once was? Once upon a time the Navy had taught her strength. It had taught her the value of Honor, Courage, and Commitment; the Navy's core values. Had she really forgotten them? Or had she just been so beaten down that she was just a shell of her former self?

A small sliver of determination took root in her soul. Carefully, she raised herself up on all fours. She would stand up even if it killed her. Finn had died bravely — on his feet. She would do the same. "Remember...," he commanded as he kicked her in the stomach. Her breath fled from her lungs. Pain blossomed as she rolled onto her side, her knees coming up to her chest. Her arms circled protectively around her. 'Don't cry. Don't cry.' She told herself to try to stop the tears. He didn't deserve to see them.

He stood over her, "I'll kill you, Ames. I swear I will." She fought the urge to vomit as he turned to go meet the sheriff's car that drove up. Just as quickly as the determination had come, it had gone. There was no where she could hide, no where that would ever be safe. Matthew would find her anywhere, there was no point in trying to hide anymore. It was going to happen whenever he wanted it to... he would kill her and there was nothing she could do about it. Soon she would be just another casualty in his rage, another 'thing' he blamed on someone else instead of taking responsibility for his own actions.

Flipping back over she crawled to Finn and Rocky. She took Finn's hand in hers. As tears rolled down her face, she swiped the blood away from his cheeks. The motion only served to smear it, which made her shake from silent sobs. Finn was dead. The last of her family was gone. She closed his eyes, letting her hand rest for a moment. Rage burned within her, but it burned with a dim flame. She was angrier at herself than Matthew. What had she ever seen in him? How could she possibly continue on? Rocky whimpered, drawing her attention. She reached up and cupped his muzzle. Finn was gone, but he loved that dog... she would take care of him, for Finn.

"Evening, how're things?" Matthew's disarming attitude screamed that something was off.

The deputy climbed partially out of his car, his eyes wide with disbelief. Amy knew that he had seen Finn's body. Things like this just didn't happen here, in this small town. "What's going on here?"

"The dog was off the leash. I was just walking past, isn't that right, Jer?"

Jer nodded, "Yep, that's right."

"The dog tried to attack us. I did the only thing I could. I fired my weapon, which I have a permit for, at the dog. Looks like I accidentally hit his owner though." As Matthew got close to the Sheriff's deputy he pulled the gun that he had used to shoot Finn with out. "Isn't that what happened, Jer?"

"Yep, sure is. Isn't it, Deputy?"

The Deputy looked back and forth from them to her, "Um..." His hand was still on the door to his cruiser. Unfortunately, he had never pulled his weapon, so he was at a loss against two guys with guns. Such an idiotic newbie move.

"Deputy, this is what's going to happen. Jer and I, we are going to walk away scot free. Our names, appearances, etc aren't even going to be mentioned in your report." He pointed to her, "She'll keep her mouth shut and you get to live. How's that?" The Deputy tried to take a step back. His eyes grew wider. "Deputy, I could just as easily kill you too… Put your hands up." He did as he was told and Matthew stepped forward. Grabbing the gun from the Deputy's holster he turned back towards her and Finn. "Ames, if you care about that dog then you'll get him."

Grabbing at Rocky's collar, she tried to drag him away. Rocky fought her, twisting and turning, trying to loosen her hold so he could continue to protect Finn. "Rocky…" she begged. Finally, she was able to get him to move. He snarled and jerked towards Matthew. Dogs knew when people were evil. Maybe if she had been paying more attention she would have seen what Rocky had before she fell for Matthew, before all of the events were set into motion.

She had only gotten Rocky a few feet away when Matthew, standing next to Finn's feet, raised the gun at Finn's body. "You see, Ames, the trick is to shoot in the same path of the bullet. The other one was a thru and thru. This one just has to do the same thing. That's the joy of using standard police caliber weapons. You know the size will be the same." He fired the gun into Finn's chest. The jerk of his dead body caused her to jump, a scream caught in her throat. Turning back to her he grinned, "The tracks will match and no one will know. No one will be able to prove anything different."

CHAPTER 2

Six months later

ALEC MACDANIEL'S HANDS TIGHTLY GRIPPED the steering wheel of the fancy sports car. "Take deep breaths," he whispered to himself. "Tis no one to be harmed here. Tis no need to protect anyone." He released a deep breath on a sad sigh, "There tis no one to watch die."

Staring out, he took in the area around him. The small cottage resided on a plot of land on the edge of the small town of New Hope, that bordered a forest. The early morning frost gave off a steamy sort of fog that rolled through the air, making it hard to see what was right on the ground. When it rolled around to late afternoon, that frost that had long since burnt off revealed short grass, tall southern pine trees, and a few deer that were courageous enough to wander through the small forest close to the sparse homes that bordered it. Most people lived close to town, so it was always quiet. Solitude was something he prized.

Unfortunately, this was a different sort of trip, not like his past ones — vacations and trips of renewal. It could be said that this was an attempt to flee the terrors of the night. The tongues had yet to cease wagging at him back home. In fact, some said he was running away. Others said he was more guilty than the man that pulled the trigger. Loss was something terrible when it took the people you loved, but was even worse when it was your fault.

The cottage belonged to a friend of an old friend — one that didn't blame him for Morvena, one that did not believe he should be over her death less than a year after... Breaths began coming in short gasps as he slipped into his memories, the ones that would forever haunt him.

His gaze drifted to his hands, the same hands that had been coated in her blood — the blood of his wife... A hit. His wife had been killed because of him, because of his job.

Shaking his head to clear the memories, he brought himself back to the present. The hands gripping the steering wheel as if it was a life line, were no longer drenched in blood. He had scrubbed them enough to know that nothing remained. It took effort to remove his hands from their death grip. Focusing on the cabin once again, he reached to open the door. The middle of nowhere was as good a place as any to spend his suspension. His indefinite suspension...

Alec scrubbed at his face, the 12 o'clock shadow rough against his palms. Even though Morvena had never followed him on his American vacations while she was alive, she haunted his every step since. If only he had been home more, then maybe she would still be alive. Maybe the baby would be too, even if it wasn't his.

Stepping out of the car, he grinned at the cool moist air. Not as cool as Scotland, of course, but still beautiful in its own rite.

As he walked up the porch steps the top one creaked under his weight. He gave a sad grin. It would be harder for anyone to sneak up on him with a creaky step. You could leave the Yard, but the Yard never really left you. The skills necessary to be a good inspector became ingrained. They were never forgotten, although sometimes they just weren't enough to save the ones you loved.

As he opened the door he took a deep breath. It was like walking into a zone of safety once he crossed the threshold, as if the bad things were trapped just outside the door. Hopefully the nightmares would not follow him inside either. It had been so long since he had slept a full night... One day he might even be able to forgive himself, if he did not see it so often.

Closing the heavy wooden door he let his hand linger on the old brass doorknob. It felt rough beneath his fingers, it's age evident. Taking a deep breath he felt at peace. The smell of the cedar chair rails that lined the entryway brought peace to him. It reminded him of the cedar rocking chair his grandda' had back home in Scotland. Alec could almost hear the steady rocking of the chair. Thump. Thump. Thump. As it glided back and forth, lightly striking the floor. Oh, how he missed his family when he was away from them.

First, a call home was needed. It would do him good to hear his family's voices. He took off his black leather biker jacket and threw it on the small black leather sofa. His midnight blue t-shirt was tucked into his blue jeans and when added with the boots he was wearing created the perfect bad boy image, it screamed for him to be left alone.

Alec sighed deeply as he turned and went outside to sit on the porch swing. It groaned slightly under him. The wood was old and warped, but still good. He pulled out his cell phone and dialed his brother Rory. Upon the third ring he was greeted with a gruff, "What!"

Alec grinned at his brother's usual way of answering the phone. It never was a question, but instead an unerring annoying demand to know who would dare interrupt his fishing from the famous limestone lochs of Assyant north of Ullapool towards Elphin. It was Rory's forced vacation time. Every year the poor Constable was forced to take a vacation. Every year he spent it fishing. Alec could practically see the look of exasperation on Rory's face at the ringer on his phone scaring away all the fish. It was some song about dogs if he remembered correctly. He asked, "'Tis that anyway to greet your eldest brother, lad?"

He was answered with a laugh, "Should have known. Yer the only fool to interrupt a man's business."

Alec smiled at their banter and asked, "A business ye say?"

"Aye, a business…Not like that fancy car habit of yers," Rory jousted.

Alec laughed, "Rory, I miss ye somethin' terrible when I'm gone. Yer the only one who can cheer me up." He always enjoyed passing insults with his brother Rory.

"Well, dear brother of mine, Mum would love for ye to come back home. Ian will be back by the end of next week." Of course, family was expected to help with the guests that would be arriving.

"Aye, that lad just had to go get an education in London," Alec joked, knowing they were all proud of Ian for getting his Business degree, as all the MacDaniels were required to attend college whether they made use of it or not. Their mother had even insisted that Rory take some form of classes to get a degree even when it was destined that he fish his life away. Ironically, it turned out their mother had been right. Despite their troubled youth as the town pranksters, each MacDaniel son, except Ian, ended up getting a degree that was geared towards law enforcement. Alec had ended up at Scotland Yard, Rory as a local constable, Tavish as a bodyguard for an exclusive protection agency, and… Danny joined the military. The loss of Danny had taken their family by surprise, but their mother refused to believe that he was gone. Just missing — missing in the desert.

"That he did…Oh, Mum's been fashed somethin' terrible about how her oldest is neigh thirty and without a wife to show him happiness," his brother warned.

Alec groaned, their mother had decided a few months ago that Alec was done mourning and had taken it upon herself to find him a new wife. She had never liked Morvena, but refused to say so to Alec as she thought he loved her. "Not again," he whispered, "I thought she was done when she tried to set me up with Mary from ole' Duncan's garage." He lifted his legs and let the swing go hoping the rocking movement from the swing would soothe him.

A laugh greeted his ears, "Aye, Mary!" His brother's delighted revelry always seemed to come at his expense. "The lass dinnae even know the whole of it! She kept a tinkerin' with the car and Mum was so fashed!"

The memory brought a smile to Alec's face as well. Mary had definitely ignored his mother and her host of mysterious car issues over a two month timespan. Two months. That's how long it took her to give up on Mary. Had she found someone else?

"Aye, that we all did. I'm just glad it's ye she's focused her matchmaking on, not me. I dinnae intend to settle down for a wee bit longer; too many fish in the loch."

Alec smiled knowing that Rory was not speaking of women, but instead the brown trout he loved so much. The smile was dimmer than it used to be though. Soon Rory would find a wife. Soon he would have a family. Then his other brothers would as well. Too much had been lost already. Between Morvena and his older brother, Alec was not sure if he would be able to find happiness again. Happiness came with too high of a price. "Rory, I need ye to do me a favor. I need ye to take the heat off of me."

"What do ye mean?"

"Find someone, for Mum's sake. Get 'er to focus on ye, so I can grieve. I dinnae know if I will ever be ready again."

A deep sigh came through the phone. "Alec, the shootin' was not yer fault."

"Dinnae," he replied sharply. He could not handle one more person saying it was not his fault. Not one more person saying their condolences or telling him to move on. If they did he was going to punch something.

Rory seemed to get the hint. "Well, lad, I've got to get back to my line as I believe I may be ignoring the wee fishes. Give us a call when yer flyin' in and we'll pick ye up."

"Aye, love ye, Rory, and catch a beaut' for me." Alec hung up feeling better about being so far away from home. Maybe he really just needed time to get away for a bit, time to bask in the glow of silence. He looked out over the fields and sighed. The sun was just beginning to set and cast a beautiful golden glow across the tall grass near the tall pine trees. It was far different from home, but it was comfortable. He was about to go back inside when he heard a shrill scream through the woods on the right side of the house. He jumped up and listened.

When he heard it again he took off towards the sound.

CHAPTER 3

AMY WAS FURIOUS. LOOKING UP, towards the ground, she cringed. Rocky was fanatically barking at her, that kind of barking where he was so excited that he was spazzing out. "Hush!" Her demand to cease was met with even more enthusiasm as he began jumping around in circles, enjoying the game they were playing. The only problem she had with this came in the tiny, seemingly insignificant detail that this was definitely not a game and she was definitely not happy about it.

Wailing around, she screamed in frustration before uttering a string of expletives as she hung upside down ten feet in the air because some idiotic poacher had left a trap out on her property. Her property of all places! The very idea made her blood boil. Poachers… She despised them. They had no business being anywhere near her or her land.

Of course, she would not be in this mess to begin with if Rocky had not jerked the leash out of her hand. Therefore, it all came back to Rocky.

The Hound from Hell.

Her eyes narrowed. Upon him looking at her, he knew he was in trouble. His ears went down and his tail went between his legs. Yep, he knew he was in trouble all right. Rocky bounded a few steps away and sat down, still barking — quieter, but still barking. Stubborn little thing. Oddly, it was like he took after her in that regard.

"You stupid mutt!" She glared offensively at the playful boxer. Shaking her fists at him, "When I get down from here I am going to skin you alive! When I'm done with that, I'm going to donate your fur to the Humane Society." She scowled at him. "Just for the Hell of it!" Rocky hopped up, wagging his tail ferociously. There were times when she swore it moved at superhero speeds.

Rocky knew she would never hurt him though, making all of her threats absolutely meaningless. Thinking about the day Finn died, her eyes began to tear up. The pup still missed Finn. When they visited his grave, Rocky would lay down and whine. It was as if he knew Finn was buried there, buried and never coming back. There was no way Rocky would ever come to harm at her hands, not when they both missed Finn.

Ignoring him, Amy blew out a heavy breath as she tried to calmly assess her situation. She looked up at her left foot and reached to undo the rope around her ankle. Unfortunately, the poacher had not tied it correctly and the slip knot came loose before she could even grab it. She screamed as she fell, slamming her eyes shut as the air whooshed around her. It came as a surprise when upon hitting the ground it was somewhat softer than she expected and went "Oof!"

Keeping her eyes tightly shut she waited; however, the pain did not come. The ground felt like it was moving.

It was! She opened her eyes, looking at the clouds above, as the ground moved beneath her again. "Lass, what were ye doin' hangin' from a rope?" The deep voice startled her. Cocking her head to the side, she looked behind her at the source of the voice. Her stomach dropped at what she saw.

Amy was lying on top of a beautiful man. In fact, he was the most beautiful man she had ever met. Her first thought was that he should be on the cover of a romance novel. Her second thought was that if he was she would definitely make the time to read it, and she was a woman that didn't make time for much outside of work. His icy blue eyes caused her heart to speed up and her lungs refused to take in air. For the first time in two years she felt a spark of something. Not sure what it was a spark of, but she knew it was important to be wary of. Sparks were dangerous.

Amy was drawn out of her reverie by his accent. "What did you just say?" Her voice sounded odd to her, whimsical and besotted. His eyes were so intense that they had her drowning in them. The brilliant blue reminded her of the sky over the ocean when she was out to sea, not a cloud in the sky, no worries, no drama. Just free, open, blue sky for as far as the eye could see.

Dragging herself out his gaze, she noticed he was frowning at her. Even without knowing him at all, she could say that the frown looked foreign upon his face. In fact, there were permanent laugh lines around his eyes that confirmed it.

"I asked if yer noggin' is alright. Ye seem to be a bit out of it." His voice was cautious, as if he expected her to be of some sort of danger to him.

Amy felt mysteriously drawn to his lips and found herself casually wondering what they would taste like. However, common sense finally decided to make a re-appearance, just in the nick of time too.

Ugh! Stupid. Has it really been that long? Hormones were screaming at her as she realized she was still lying on top of him. Rolling off of him she tried to cover her blush by getting angry. It was too much to be attracted to him with what all was going on in her life. There was finally a chance for her to save herself, so no one else got hurt, and here she was ogling at some guy. Some very very attractive guy, but still…

Still in a crouch she frowned, "Dude, I don't know where you think you're at, but I sure as hell can't understand what you're saying." She stood up trying to gain the advantage. "You need to learn proper English if you're gonna' hang around here."

"Alec."

"Hn?"

"Alec, tis my name." Alec frowned and pushed himself up off the ground. As he dusted himself off, she took a step back. He was tall. Tall and even more gorgeous than she though. "I am speakin' English."

She made a face and pointed a finger at him, "I said proper."

"Lass, yer missin' a tool or two…"

Anger boiled deep in her gut. How dare he… "Excuse me? Did you just imply that I'm not all there?" She crossed her arms over her chest and raised an eyebrow, daring him to confirm it. At his arrogant nod her temper became strained. Amy uncrossed her arms and balled her fists at her sides. Her mouth opened as if to say something then closed thinking better of it. This would definitely be much more fun than letting her anger get the better of her. A smile graced her lips and before he could realize what she was doing she pushed him back. Then the dog got underneath his feet, tripping him.

As he landed on his back on the hard ground he looked up to see her towering over him. Good. Now she had the advantage. *Don't show fear*, she told herself. *Act like a*

Siren. Yeah, Siren's are all powerful. In what she suspected was full on Siren mode she leaned forward just a bit. Placing one hand on her hip, tossing in a bit of sass, she narrowed her eyes. With the other hand she pointed a long, thin finger at him. Appear threatening, it will keep him from getting involved.

"Let me tell you somethin', bud, around here I am definitely not the person you want to mess with." She used the finger that had been pointing at him and jerked it towards her head, "I can assure you that everything's fine upstairs." How dare he imply otherwise! "And, just so you know, the rope was from a poacher trying for game." Taking a step back, she crossed her arms over her chest. "I don't know where you're from," Seeing his mouth open, as if to answer, she slung out her hand really quickly to make a halting motion, "and I really don't care. This is your only warning to stay away from me, got it?"

Without waiting for a response, she turned and walked away, only making it a few feet before realizing that Rocky wasn't following. He was standing right beside the guy, not moving an inch. The man turned his head slowly as Rocky whined and faced the seventy-five pound dog, which promptly licked him on the cheek. Amy whistled a shrill whistle which caused Rocky to turn his head towards her. Slapping a hand against her thigh, he then bounded off towards her. She watched with narrowed eyes as the guy pushed himself up off the ground.

Staring in her direction, he shook his head. "As if bein' here wasn't enough, I had to go meet a loon," he muttered just loud enough for her to hear. He shook his head again as he began walking back in the direction he had run. "I should have stayed in Ullapool where no loons are runnin' amuck, although," He paused and turned his head to glance once again in her direction, "here they have quite bonnie loons." He smiled despite the obvious soreness from her landing on him and taking him to the ground with her.

There was no fit response to his antics. Her mouth opened and closed. No words were good enough, so she turned and fled with Rocky hot on her heels. While fleeing the scene, Amy muttered all the way back to her one bedroom cabin. "How dare that jerk think I'm freaking missing something upstairs!" Rocky barked at her heels, still animated from the excitement of meeting the stranger. Amy looked down at him, "This is all your fault you crazy mutt." Rocky wagged his tail at her in hopes of being rewarded for playing the game so well and reached up to lick her hand. She jerked her hand back rapidly, "Just because I got stuck with you doesn't mean that I have to like you. In fact, I don't like you not one little bit. You're just lucky that I feel sorry enough for you to feed you daily." That was far from the truth. Amy actually liked the dog very much, but felt better not admitting it to anyone, not even herself.

The footfalls echoed loudly as she stalked up the four steps to the door, making each and every stomp count. Rocky pushed past her inside and after she entered she slammed it shut. A few pictures on the wall rattled and one fell. She heard glass shatter and grimaced. She went and picked it up almost crying when she saw which picture had fallen. "Oh no…" It was a picture of her mother, father, brother, and her at her Boot Camp graduation in Great Lakes, Illinois. She was in her dress whites and her parents were both casting proud looks at her. It was the only picture she had of them all together. Her parents had been killed six months later, but her brother had neglected to tell her for another year after they had died. He said he had wanted her to be able to concentrate on her job over in Iraq instead of mourning for them. Each time she had called or emailed he'd say they were out or that they couldn't figure out the computer. Both were highly plausible, so she hadn't worried… Finn was always the big brother, always protecting her, even if it cost him… Even if it cost him his life. Best not to think about that now. The time would come soon that he would be avenged.

Amy grabbed a small trashcan to put the broken pieces of glass in as her phone rang. Rocky barked incessantly, growing shriller with each ring. On the fourth ring the answering machine finally picked it up. "Hey, this is Amy's answering machine. That should give you a clue to the fact that I'm not here right now, but if you feel up to leaving a message go ahead, it can't hurt. I might even feel up to giving you a call back." She smirked at her voice.

"Amy, you will give me a call back." Her breath caught. A pounding began in her chest, faster and faster it went. Fear. Unadulterated fear filled her at the sound of that voice. "The number hasn't changed." He took a deep breath as if he could inhale the very scent of her fear from wherever he was. "I do so miss your voice, and the feel of your body… It drives me mad." Her eyes went wide and her breathing became erratic as the voice continued. "Amy, why did you run from me? You know the drugs do crazy things to me. I need you by my side." Knees buckling she leaned against the wall. "You really should call me back, after all, we're still married. I know you're there. In fact, I know a lot more than you think…"

As she sunk to the ground the machine cut off. Crouched in the corner amidst the broken glass she wept.

Rocky sat beside her growling at the offending machine. Her crying turned to a keening sound as she wrapped her arms around his neck. "Good dog," she whispered on a choked sob.

It did no good calling the police. The Deputy had kept silent. He had proclaimed his innocence, but he was just as guilty as Matthew, if not more so. No one would find the dishonorably discharged Navy SWC. He had promised to kill her. No one would help. No one could help. It was too late to tell the DEA that Matthew had been involved in the death of her brother — too late to tell them that was why she ran. It was too late to tell them Matthew's greatest secret. Why tell anyways? It just got people killed. The last person that had tried to help her had been killed. He had been murdered in cold blood and it was all her fault. All of it was her fault.

CHAPTER 4

THE NEXT MORNING ALEC WAS standing with his friend Nancy inside a place called Lilly's Books, "Alec, Lilly Cadera is graciously allowing you to stay in her cabin, so you better act like you enjoy it and be nice."

Nancy had been Alec's best friend in college, never steering him wrong. She had even tried to warn him about Morvena, but he had not listened to her.

"Alright, Nancy, this is me havin' a laugh," he made a face that one could interpret as a smile before Nancy rolled her eyes at him. "Och, lass, yer too uptight."

"Alec, I don't think you truly understand just how hard it was to get Lilly to agree to rent out her cabin to you. This time of year it can be rented out for a lot of money. Besides Lilly is a good friend of mine, so please behave. She used to work with me at the agency. When it went belly up we both went our separate ways, though we stayed in touch." Nancy smoothed down her ruffled skirt as she continued to speak, "Lilly just wanted to meet you. She wants to make sure the cabin is to your liking."

"Ye could 'ave asked that over the phone." It was true. Nancy could have, but Alec sensed there was a reason that devious woman had wanted him to come in person.

"Just pretend like you're happy for five minutes. Please?"

Fine. He would pretend that he was happy, but it didn't mean that he had to like it. Alec sighed and turned away to check out his surroundings, "Tis a verra nice cabin."

He gave her a look and she threw her hands up in the air, "Alec MacDaniel, you are driving me insane. You should be excited, not looking like you're about to walk a plank."

Excited about what? How could he be excited? Life was just changing way too fast. It was hard being excited when all you could think about was someone you loved, and lost.

———— 🦓 ————

Wondering down the aisles of books he saw the true crime section, something that had once been a joy to him — stopping criminals and making them pay for their crimes. The aisle seemed to glare at him, screaming his failures like a banshee wailing in the wind. Books on murder, mayhem, drugs, terrorism, etc all lined the shelves, famous in all their painful glory. Would it ever get easier? So far the wound was still a gut wrenching one. True, it did not hurt as much as it once did, but it still served as a constant reminder of his failure.

He looked up, across the store, when he heard a knock on the glass window and Lilly Cadera ran to open the door. He listened as a familiar voice said, "Lilly, what's up with opening so late today?'

Lilly flashed a smile at the woman Alec recognized from the night before, "Hey, Amy, my friend Nancy is in town. She brought a guy too: Alec MacDaniel, a Scottish Highlander. His looks alone are going to be bringing in the masses to my store. Bored housewives are going to be fanning themselves with books saying, "Ah, Alec MacDaniel is a fine specimen of man," for the next few months if they find out he's here, so we're opening late today."

He heard a laugh and thought that it sounded remarkable, "Lilly, I think you're exaggerating just a tiny bit."

"No, I'm not…" Her eyes were wide and Amy wondered just what was going on. "Well, we're opening late because my friend's in town and it's been forever since I've seen her. I'm not exaggerating about Alec, take a look for yourself…" Lilly pointed over at him and Amy's face changed. Her eyes widened and her jaw dropped. She was speechless.

Alec flashed her a grin. "Well, if it's not the loon." He noticed that the white t-shirt she wore had a picture of a bride and a male stripper running away from a groom and a caption that read 'The bachelorette party was too much fun.' He also noticed that her jeans were slung low on her hips and that the sweatshirt she had tied around her waist only emphasized it. He fleetingly wondered what was in the backpack she had with her. Was she in school?

He was certain that his devil of a grin caused a ripple of under current to run through her stomach. He wore a similar outfit to the one he had worn last night, except now he was wearing a slate gray button up dress shirt, with the sleeves rolled up, and dark dress slacks. At least, he assumed that he was affecting her by the way her breath hitched for a second before she seemed to realize what he had said.

Then Amy glared at him. It was not just any type of glare either. It could have peeled the ten layers of paint off of his parent's attempt at a nursery for Ian. His mother had been convinced Ian would be a girl. His father had been convinced that Ian was a boy. They each sneaked in the room and painted over the colors until the week before Ian was born. His mother had thrown in the towel, said she changed her mind on the colors. The tears in her eyes had told a different story though. His father had painted it pink again in the middle of the night for her, Alec had helped. As a result, Ian had a pink room until he was twelve. It had never bothered him, but he received never-ending teasing from his brothers. Alec smiled at the memory.

Amy's eyes narrowed and her lips were pushed together into a pencil thin line. "Well, if isn't the jerk."

Nancy and Lilly both looked confused, "um… have you two met?"

Alec opened his mouth to answer, but was stopped by his cell phone ringing. He pulled it from his pocket and opened it, "Yes?"

"Och, my dear Alec, why hasn't my own sweet lad called his poor mum?"

Alec's smile came out in full force. "Ah, my dear sweet sainted mum, the one who is fashed because her oldest is neigh thirty and without a wife?"

"Alec Kirk MacDaniel, dinna take that sassy tone with me." Alec resisted a cheeky response. "My own son…"

"Mum, I love ye, ye know I do. I called Rory to let him know I made it."

"Aye, but not yer mum. The lass that suffered the pains of child birth for yer sorry hide."

"The same mum who told me that if my plane fell into the ocean it would serve me right for leavin'?"

There was silence on the other end. "Lad, what did ye say to yer mum? She looks 'bout to cry." His father's voice provided comfort, but sadness at the words.

Alec's playful spirit deserted him at the thought of his mother crying because of what he said, "I dinna mean it."

"Alec, no son of mine will be a wanker. Ye better straighten out yer head or come home so I can box ye upside it. Now, how did yer travels go?"

"Quite well, Da'. I should be done 'round the time Ian comes home from England for break."

"Speakin' of yer brother," he whispered, "he's in trouble with yer mum."

In the background Alec heard, "Alan MacDaniel, don't ye be spreadin' gossip! I want that runt home, so I can box his ears in myself!"

"What did Ian do, Da'?"

His father spoke quietly into the phone, "that brat pulled a prank on yer mum and she's none too happy 'bout it. I'll tell ye more later, but for now she's givin' me the evil eye. Keep yer wife happy or eat yer supper elsewhere... Love ye, Son."

Alec hung up with a smile on his face. His youngest brother Ian was a bit of a prankster. They all were really, so there's no telling what he did to their mother. Ian just happened to be the most creative, although, since he was the youngest he was also the safest from their mother's anger. When he looked up he noticed Lilly and Nancy were still waiting for an explanation. Amy was gone.

CHAPTER 5

AMY SLID HER SWEATSHIRT OVER her head as she walked into the office, angrily whispering curse words as she saw the numbers on the clock. Well, there was a first time for everything. Dropping her backpack at her feet, she plopped down in the chair behind the rental desk. Quickly signing in, she held her breath. He was sure to notice. Nothing made it past Dylan James. Nothing.

The chair scraped against the tile floor… Turning around she smiled, preparing herself for what was to come. Her boss hung his head out of his office, "Amy, you're late?" He sounded more shocked than anything. Amy surmised it was because she had never ever been late before.

She shrugged, "I'm sorry. I went over to ask Lilly if those books about Costa Rica had come in or not, but she's got some fancy guy over there. I'll head back once he's gone and check on it though."

Dylan leaned against the doorframe of his office. The flannel shirts he wore made him seem more like a lumberjack than the owner of an outdoor equipment rental company. However, today was apparently not a flannel shirt day. "Why do I get the feeling that you're not too excited about this 'fancy guy'?" He stepped further out of his office and she barely suppressed a grin at his flamboyant Hawaiian shirt.

Holding back a laugh she croaked out, "Are we advertising the Hawaii trip today?"

"Hey, now. My wife brought this back from her business trip in Oahu. It would hurt her feelings if I didn't wear it."

"You're such a good husband," the grin was in full force now. Dylan James was a man madly in love with his wife. That is why he was safe. That was why she still worked here when her skills could put her working for major firms. Well, it was one of the reasons. Dylan James always had everyone's best interests at heart. Amy suspected that at one time he had been a vastly different man, but that was before Marie. Marie had changed him, for the better.

"Of course I am. Why would I be anything else? I'll let you in on a secret." He shifted his face into a deadly serious look. There was no telling what he would say next as he leaned forward in what could be best described as a conspiratorial confession. "I screwed up quite a bit while Marie and I were dating." Amy rolled her eyes. "Now quit stalling and answer the question."

Amy once again rolled her eyes. Dylan was such a kidder, but could never be distracted from his ultimate purpose. "Fine. Because I met him last night and he accused me of having a screw loose."

Silence greeted her. A look of shock passed over Dylan's face before he threw back his head and laughed. The laugh was a deep boisterous thing, full of joy. It lacked the condescension she had come to expect from people over the years. In fact, Dylan's laugh was purely from amusement. Not at her though. He would never laugh at her. "The guy called you crazy?" She nodded. "And he's still alive?" She nodded again and her boss laughed even harder. "To think I never thought I would see the day that you would let someone talk to you like that."

Amy frowned, thinking back on the last seven months. It was true that she had stayed away from the other workers. They had seemed to understand her need to ignore them, but her boss thought it gave him a reason to pry. In the end they had struck up a casual friendship. He knew more about her than anyone else, yet he was still in the dark about so much. He was right though, it was a rare thing indeed when she let someone speak to her as she had the Scot. "Dylan, it's not funny. The guy was a jerk and I can barely understand him because of that dang accent."

"What accent?"

"I swear the guy acts like he's from Scotland or something."

"Well, now, isn't that where you've always wanted to go?" Still leaning against the doorframe, he gave a wink.

"That's beside the point. You have no idea how embarrassing it was! I mean, I was staring at him like I was a freaking crazy lady and he... Why are you grinning?"

"Because, dear Amy, your life is about to change." He took a deep sigh, "Did I ever tell you about how I met my wife?"

Before Amy could answer the phone began ringing, interrupting their conversation. She held up a finger signaling for him to hold that thought. "Blazing Outdoors, Amy speaking, how may I help you?"

"Amy Killigan?"

She instantly grew wary. No one ever asked for her by name. No one. "Yes?" Had he found her already? Her home number was easy to find, the location of her home progressively harder to find, but there was nothing, at all, that connected her to Blazing Outdoors. Not even an I-9. Her boss let her work under the table and never asked why. He would be screwed if the IRS found out.

There was a sigh from the person on the other end of the line, "Mrs. Killigan, this is Sheriff Leann Newcastle of the Hope County Sheriff's Department. I'm calling in reference to your brother's murder seven months ago."

Amy knew that one day someone would ask. Someone would be interested. Someone would want to discuss what had happened... So many people had come and gone the day he died. The neighbors had fired off weapons that same day, maybe if theyn't then the deputy would have been more prepared for the sight that greeted him upon driving up to the house. Not long before Matthew had shown up, the deputy had first tried to give her brother a ticket. He tried to give Finn a ticket for Rocky being off of a leash. Then when he showed up again... Well, instead of calling for help, Matthew had gotten to him.

Taking a deep breath she decided to play dumb with the Sheriff. It would be better if no one knew that her ex-husband had called her. They'd ask questions. Questions were dangerous. Questions were even more dangerous when they had the ability to cost someone their life. The killing had to stop. "Did you guys finally find the prick that killed him?" Although, there could be another reason for the Sheriff to call. She felt hope creep into her for the first time in so long. Maybe they had caught Matthew. Maybe he had finally screwed up enough to where they would go after him and she would be free.

Maybe she would not need her plan after all.

"Ma'am, we did find one of the two suspects, yes.

However, we only found his body. Jerry Carver, the suspect, was shot five times and left for dead at one of the local rock quarries. His face was beyond recognition, so the identification is not confirmed, but we found his wallet on the scene. We should have confirmation in a few hours. I just wanted to let you know first. Unfortunately, there were no witnesses, so we don't really have any leads at this moment. We're looking into it though. I'm sorry. I truly am. I know you wanted to have your day in court..."

Amy felt tears prick her eyes; she wanted to have something else with the bastard. Not a day in court, but it was better the Sheriff not know what she wanted. Someone else just happened to do the dirty work for her and she just happened to know who. "Yes, but he got the same death he gave to my brother. I guess that's a form of justice isn't it?"

"Ma'am, normally I wouldn't say this, but the suspect did get what he deserved. Once again, I am really sorry and I know you're still grieving for your brother. On a side note, the officer that gave your brother the ticket before his death was suspended without pay for the last six months and today was the first day of his termination."

"Yeah, but he'll probably get a job as a cop somewhere else." They always did. People that broke the law never paid for it. Or at least not that she had seen.

That thought gave her pause. Was she becoming jaded? Had it truly been that long since she had seen something to give her hope that everything would be alright?

"No, he won't. We've put a permanent black mark on his record and no one will hire him. I'm personally going to make sure everyone knows that he's responsible for the death of a civilian. He should have done his job protecting you and your brother instead of protecting a criminal."

Just how much had he finally come out and told them? The day of the murder he had clammed shut, refusing to tell even the slightest of details. The other officers on the scene had chalked it up to shock from witnessing his first crime scene. Amy had known better though. Matthew could put fear in anyone. It never left, not even when he was no longer around. It was a long term thing with Matthew, hunting his prey until they thought they were safe, then coming out of the woodworks to scare them again. Fear was a terrible thing... Absolutely terrible. It tends to take over your life, every aspect, until you do not even recognize your own self anymore, until you were too far gone to return to the person you were before. "Thank you, Sheriff. I sincerely appreciate the call."

"You're welcome, but there was another reason for my call today...Is your husband's full name Matthew Daemon Killigan?"

Amy's throat went dry and her stomach clenched in fear. "Yes, why?" Scenarios flew through her mind about why the Sheriff would be asking, none of them ending happily for her. His name alone brought back all of the fears she had spent years trying to quell. He was still hunting her, coming out of the woodwork to scare her yet again.

"I just wanted to give you a heads up; he murdered an officer in San Diego, California. A DEA Agent. It's believed that he might be coming this way."

"Uh... Thank you for letting me know. I appreciate it." Taken aback at the Sheriff's cautious tone it was hard for her to get the words out. Was the Sheriff actually trying to do her job? Was she going to try to protect her?

It was unexpected to her for someone to care enough to warn her of his presence. So many different reasons for her warning came to mind. Some good, but some were self-serving on the part of the Sheriff. Maybe she just wanted to prove that her deputies were able to obey the law, that they could be trusted. Well, Amy was not about to help them with that. It was too late for that. She had other plans.

"If I were you I would take off for a while until we can track him down."

It was too late for that too. He would find her no matter where she went, she knew that better than anyone. No one would protect her. They could not stand up to him. "There's no point. He was a SWC, that's like Special Forces for the Navy; he'll find me no matter where I am." Maybe it was time, time for her to save herself. Could she be brave enough to do it, to do what needed to be done?

"I can arrange for a Deputy to drive past your place every once in a while if you would like." The tone of the Sheriff's voice was hopeful. It was almost as if she was extending an olive branch, trying to make up for the past.

"No, that's okay. I'll be fine, but thank you for the offer." The fewer people that knew where she lived the better and safer for her it would be. It would also give her time to put her plan into action. So many years now. So many years of planning and plotting. It was finally time.

No heroes were coming to save her. They were all gone.

It was time for her to be her own hero. It was time for her to try to save herself. At least, then maybe she would be able to live with herself, even if Matthew succeeded in killing her.

"Okay, then have a good day Mrs. Killigan. Please stay safe."

"You too, Sheriff." Amy hung up the phone with a mind numbing terror gripping her. Fleeting thoughts went through her brain as she began to hyperventilate.

So much to do. So little time. He was coming for her. She had to find him first. She grabbed her backpack and slung it over her shoulder. It was time, time to put a stop to it, time to be her own savior, time to right what was wrong.

"Amy?"

Ignoring him, she didn't say anything as she ran for the door. Fear caused her to run on autopilot, striving for safety. Safety was paramount, but running on auto-pilot put her at odds with reason. She could not focus long enough to retain any of the thoughts running through her mind, much less explain her fear to anyone.

It was easier to run, run to safety, hide from the danger coming for her. No one could save her from him. Yet, there came a time in everyone's life when running did no good. It only put off the inevitable. The time for running and hiding was over. It was time for her to take charge and do what no one else would. Maybe then she could live with herself. Maybe then she could live with the damage she had caused.

CHAPTER 6

ALEC LOOKED UP FROM THE cash wrap to see Amy running out of the store next door to a black Jeep Wrangler in the parking lot Blazing Outdoors and Lilly's Books shared. Something was wrong. He watched as she threw her bag in before she hopped in. She started it and drove off before checking to see if anyone was coming. It was possible that she was just a really bad driver, but the look on her face… He recognized it and wondered about it. It was a look of pure unadulterated fear. It was a look that should never be upon a woman's face.

He was not sure why, but for some reason it made him angry to see that look on hers. It struck him deep within, his long dormant heart beating a tiny cadence of beats. Maybe it was his Scottish ancestry. Maybe it was the way he was raised. Maybe it was the job he held too long. He could't take the thought of that look would remaining on her face. Alec vowed to find out who put that look upon her face. When he found them he would make them rue the day they ever met her, much less hurt her.

"Lilly," he added an extra lilt to his voice, "who is the lass ye spoke to earlier?"

"You mean Amy?"

Amy, thinking of the meaning of her name he smiled. It fit her well. "Please tell me about her?"

"Amy?" Lilly's nose scrunched up. The look of confusion was only momentary. Her eyes went round. "Amy!?! Really?"

Alec gulped. The look she gave him was one of a warrior planning a dangerous conquest, one where there was no other choice, but to succeed.

"Oh, you'll love her!"

He could see the wheels turning in her head. The plans she was making were plans of a woman on a mission, a mission of matchmaking — the Devil's Ninth Hell... "Woah! No, no, no! I am just curious. Tis all."

Alec gulped as she grinned. "You may be curious now, but you will be something else before long. She is awfully pretty isn't she?"

"Um..." He slowly backed up until he hit something. Several paperback books rained down upon him.

Nancy's laugh brought him up short. Turning towards her, he saw that she was immersed in a book by her favorite author. "Oh, Alec knows she's pretty. He's Scottish after all. The man knows finery when he sees it. He just might need some background information, you know," she made a shooing motion, "to help him along."

Lilly grinned. Alec hung his head. The conspiracy was afoot and there was nothing that he could do about it now.

"Oh, of course. Well, she's single. At least I think she is. Never really seen her with anyone."

"Wait..." This was going too far. It had to be stopped.

"Oh, she loves tulips!"

Tulips? What did tulips have to do with it?

Nancy looked up from the book she was reading, "You could take her some tulips and ask her out! That would be so romantic!"

Sure, just like when she was hanging upside down and fell on him. Thank goodness they did not know about that. He would never hear the end of it until they had him marching down the aisle if they knew about that.

CHAPTER 7

AMY SWIPED ROUGHLY AT THE tears falling. "Stupid... Stupid! Stupid! Stupid!" She clenched the wheel harder. "How on Earth could you be so stupid! Of course they were going to find out that you knew, you freaking moron!"

She punched the wheel with her right hand. The slight pain made her feel a bit better, but she was still mad. Hell, she was pissed. Seven months and she had managed to keep quiet about who killed her brother. Even if she had been plotting revenge the whole time, she had still kept quiet about it. Then he found out where she was living now. How on Earth he found out was beyond her, but it wasn't hard with her staying in the same county. She had her landline under a different name, her house was under a different name, and she wasn't officially employed at her work. The problem was that now he knew exactly where she was. He was going to find her eventually, but she assumed that she had more time. He knew and now the stakes were higher. He was coming for her and her plan was not ready yet.

If she could lead him away from town then maybe it would not be so bad. Maybe Lilly and her boss would be safe. They were the only ones that she cared about. Maybe she could keep anyone else from getting hurt. It was time that she put a stop to this. Unfortunately, he had sworn to kill her. Not like she had much of a choice in what was going to happen. She might as well meet him out on the battlefield, at least that would show she had some honor. Honor had always been important to her. Honor, Courage, and Commitment — the Navy way. In fact, the Navy had trained her for this. Well, not this exactly, but they had trained her for how to deal with battles. There were different types of battles: some internal and some external, some involved violence, and some involved decisions. In her time she had dealt with many, this was just the most important one of her life. Taking a deep breath she resolved to do what was right and to do it with honor. It was time to fight back, time to take her life in her own hands and go after the bastard with everything she had.

With her decision made she realized that it was extremely quiet... Too quiet. She took a slow breath as she realized that her radio was off. It was never off. It never played music this far out in the boonies, but the static noise calmed her while she drove. It reminded her that she was safe...

A cold knot settled in her stomach. Risking a glance at the radio confirmed that it had indeed been turned off. Keeping her left hand on the wheel, she slowly placed her right hand in her lap. Reaching it slowly down, she pretended to drop something in the floorboard. "Oh, crap," she muttered and reached up under her seat. Expecting her hand to meet the cold trusty metal of her throwing knife, her breath caught when it wasn't there. Slowly, trying to keep her fear from showing, she sat up straight.

A voice came from behind her, "Looking for this?"

Cold metal grazed along the side of her neck. "Why don't you be a lamb and pull over for a second? We should chat, don't you think?"

She pulled over to the side of the road and came to a stop, hands stayed on the wheel. It was important for him to view her as innocent and non-threatening. "What do you want?"

"I was sent to make sure you were calm when you saw him."

Risking a glance in the mirror she recognized him. He helped Matthew... He was responsible for killing her brother, just as much as Matthew was. "You're Jerry aren't you?"

"Of course I am. Did you think he would just kill me?"

"Guess not." She shrugged slowly. "You changed a bit since the last time we met. Guess you have to when you pretend to be dead though." Being dead probably made breaking the law a little easier. It was pretty handy when no one was looking for you. "So, what's the deal?"

"Matthew didn't say. Just said that I was to make sure you stayed calm."

Still looking at him through the rearview mirror, she sighed, "You already said that." Jerry grabbed her hair and pulled her head back. A snarl graced his face. He was angry now. The calm demeanor gone.

Think fast. "I'm just saying that I don't know what's going on. Sort of in the dark here. Not fighting back. Just trying to understand." He wouldn't hurt her too much. Matthew would want her alive. The bastard always promised that he would be the one to kill her. There was no way he would let his partner have the satisfaction of being the one to kill her. That would take all of the fun out of it.

His eyes squinted, but the anger seemed to slip away a bit. Survive. That was all she needed to do. Survive him and handle Matthew. "So where are we going, Jerry?"

"He's waiting for you."

"Look, I can't drive until you tell me where I'm going. So either we sit here for the next few hours and talk about random things, or you tell me where I'm going."

Snarling, he released her hair. "Just drive."

She smirked. If he wouldn't tell her where to go that was fine. She'd find Matthew on her own when she was ready, just had to deal with Jerry first. From the looks of things, that would not be too difficult either. "Ok, Jerry, let's go." She threw it in drive and slammed on the gas. The jeep spun out as it took off, gravel slinging up behind her. Watching in the mirror, she laughed as Jerry slid around on the seats grasping rapidly for anything to hold on to. The expression on his face was hilarious! Fear and shock made his eyes and his mouth open wide. Maybe this would be fun. It sure as hell beat being scared.

"Crazy bitch! You're going to kill us both!"

"Yeah? You think so? Well, don't worry. There's a fun little curve up ahead." If she timed it just right then he would be sorry he ever got into her jeep. He would be sorry that he listened to Matthew. He would be sorry that he ever messed with her and her family.

"What are you doing!?!"

"Taking you for a drive. That is what you wanted, right?" Swerving on the small backroad, the jeep crunched over the gravel. The back end swung to the right as she drove around the sharp curve.

There it was! The curve that she needed. Jerking the wheel again she felt the knife barely miss knicking her throat.

"Stop the car! Stop the car!" His screams fell on deaf ears. There was no way that she was going to stop and give him the upper hand.

Her response was to jerk the wheel again. He couldn't be allowed to gain purchase in the back seat. If he did then there was nothing she could do. At least now while he could not keep his footing she had a chance. A small chance, but a chance.

"Why are you not listening!?! That asshole swore you would be complacent! That this would be an easy five grand!"

Her eyes flashed to the mirror. "He's paying you!?!"

"What did you think? That I was doing this for kicks?"

Some-how the knowledge that he would pay someone to hurt her hurt worse. The man that refused to buy a flashlight when his military issued one died because it cost ten cents more than the cost of a box of matches, had paid a man five grand to hurt her... Five grand! The next time it would be more. "How much did he give you to kill my brother?"

"That was just for fun."

"For fun!?! For fun!?! You son of a bitch," the words were gravely, laced with hatred. "Where is he?" Jerry did not answer her. "I'm only going to ask once more. Where. Is. He?"

"I swear I don't know! I was just supposed to get you to the bluff and knock you out! He's going to call me soon to tell me where to go from there!"

The fear on his face told her that he was telling the truth. She was amazed that he had not pissed himself. Fear did strange things to people. It seemed to make Jerry more honest.

"Then that means that I don't need you. I just need your phone..." Slamming on the brakes he flew forward and slammed against the dashboard. Keeping one hand on the wheel, she punched him in the face with her right hand. Over and over she punched him. Blood spurted from his nose and mouth. On the sixth punch he was out.

"Well, Jerry, you're not that good at fighting off a mad woman are you." He hadn't tried very hard to block at all. It seemed strange, but it was not something she wanted to take the time to consider.

Undoing her seatbelt, she reached over him and opened the passenger door. A quick search of his pockets left his cellphone in her possession. No keys though. A few tries later she had him out of the car and on to the hard round. "Guess I'll be nice and pull you to the side, so you don't get run over. I may be ex-military but I'm sort of a pushover." Once the goal was accomplished she pocketed her knife and climbed back into the jeep. Matthew would call soon. Maybe her plan would still work. The DEA may have failed, but there were still other places she could turn to, other things that she could do.

As Amy drove up to her house she was still shaking. "Focus on the plan. Just focus on the plan." Taking her hands off the wheel she shook them. She left her jeep running as she hopped out and ran to the house to get a few things that she would need. She also needed to grab Rocky from his kennel.

It never occurred to her that he was not barking like he usually did when she drove up.

She ran up the steps and threw open the door. As she stepped in she heard a noise behind her. She swung around to see what it was as something heavy hit her in the head. Pain blossomed throughout her head and her vision went wavy as she fell to the ground in a heap. A hazy figure stood over her laughing, "My dear wife, I would have thought you would have learned after the last time..." The voice drifted further away as Amy slipped into unconsciousness.

CHAPTER 8

ALEC HAD MANAGED TO FLEE from the matchmakers and get directions to Amy's house from Lilly. He had a bad feeling from deep within. Something was wrong. Call it intuition, fate, or overprotective maleness. Whatever it was, it was usually right. It was a calling deep in his soul. It had served him well over the years, especially with chasing drug runners and murderers on a daily basis. Now it was screaming for him to go after the elfin waif of a woman, screaming to the Heavens for him to find her immediately. For some reason he felt a deeply ingrained need to protect Amy from whatever it was that she was afraid of. He had no idea where this protective streak for her came from, but his father had raised him to protect a woman in trouble and that was what he was going to do. The last time he had not heeded the warning in his soul he had lost someone very important. This time he would heed it.

As he pulled into the driveway he saw Amy's jeep. The engine was still running and the door to it was open. He looked up toward the small cabin and saw a window curtain fall back into place. He took his time walking up to the front door thinking Amy would come to open it before he got there. Steeling himself for the acrid words that he knew would come from her mouth he realized that he had no excuse for being there.

Why had he not thought up an excuse on his way there? It would have been so much easier to have an excuse. Slowing his steps he waited for her. He wanted to give her a sense of control. However, when he reached the door and it remained unopened he grew concerned. "Lass, open the door. I mean ye no harm that I swear," he called out.

With the first knock the door slowly swung open, giving a slow creaking noise with it. The danger of it all suddenly shrieked at him. Something was certainly wrong. Alec whispered, "lass?" He pushed it open further, gasping at what he saw. The entire room had been ransacked and Amy lay in a crumpled heap surrounded by broken glass a few feet away.

Without thinking he rushed to her side, "lass?" He felt for a pulse and was grateful to find one. She moaned from pain as he picked her up. "Dinna worry, lass, I'm takin' ye to help." His heart constricted at the blood oozing from a wound near her left temple and from a cut on her right cheek.

Alec quickly carried her out to his rented Porsche. Carefully he put her in the passenger side. He drew the seatbelt around her. As he clipped it he tried to keep focused on getting her help. Running around to the other side of his car, he vaguely wondered where the person that had done this to her was.

He drove well above the speed limit the entire time to the hospital. She made not a sound. Even her breathing was shallow, giving an impression that there was no breath going into her lungs at all. Shakily, he reached a hand out to feel in front of her face. Relief struck him hard when he felt the moist air on the back of his hand. Strange. He had just met her, yet such relief flooded him at knowing she was alive.

He vaguely remembered where the hospital was from the map his mother had used to show him where all the necessary places were. He thought it ridiculous at the time, but now he was grateful. As he pulled up to the ambulance area of the Emergency Room he began honking his horn rapidly to get someone to come help. He cut the Porsche off and raced around the other side to get Amy from the passenger seat. A nurse came running outside to see what was going on and Alec felt relieved "Pease help her! She's been hurt!"

The nurse motioned for him to bring her in and place her on a gurney. As soon as he did he was pushed out of the way as doctors and nurses swarmed over Amy. The nurse that had told him where to put her lightly touched his arm, "Sir, don't worry, we'll help her, but first we need to know what happened."

Alec's temper was beginning to show. If they asked him one more question instead of actually helping her, he was going to lose it, "Tis just it, I dinna know. She ran earlier and looked so fashed 'bout somethin'. I went to see what had her so foxed. When I got there she was in a poor pile on the floor. Her home had been torn apart for somethin'. She was hurt."

The nurse frowned. "What's her name? Are you her next of kin?"

Alec frowned, not knowing how to handle the question of kin. "Her name is Amy," he hesitated for a second before saying, "an' I'm her fiancée." He felt bad about the little lie, but Nancy had told him stories of how American hospitals would not talk to anyone unless they were a relative, a spouse or a fiancée. He needed to know she was going to be ok. The nurse gave him a sad smile before pointing to the waiting room and he went to have a seat.

The waiting area was a small room, but it was deliriously bright. There was a flowery design on the wall. A light blue background served as the sky while the baseboards had been painted to resemble individual blades of grass. Tulips, roses, and lilies, of all colors sprung up from the grass. Clouds towards the ceiling gave the impression of a vast open sky, much like a beautiful summer day. Alec could almost smell the pollen, hear the birds painted high in the sky, and feel the wind on his skin. The painter had been very talented. Tavish would definitely have been impressed.

His musings came to an abrupt halt as his phone rang. Checking his watch, he realized that he had been waiting to hear news on her condition for fifteen minutes. "Yes?"

"Alec, my brother, it's Tavish."

Speak of the Devil… Alec ran a hang through his unruly hair, "Tavish, now is not the time. I've had a bit of trouble…"

"What happened?"

"A woman."

"Oh, the uncatchable rogue, Alec Kirk MacDaniel, has finally met his match, eh?"

"No, Tavish, I met a woman with sad doe eyes and the kind of hair a man can run his fingers through for days. A pixie little thing she is. As if the fae themselves designed her. Someone put a look of fear on her bonnie face. When I went to find out what about, the lass was hurt. Someone hurt my lass. They 'ave torn her home apart an' they 'ave beat her. It rankles my gut to think about it, Tavish."

Tavish was silent for a moment in thought before he said, "Alec, dear brother, our family has seen too much loss in the last few years. If yer lass is hurt then she is not safe there. Ye should bring her home to Ullapool where us MacDaniel's can stick together. Where we can protect yer bonnie lass."

Crossing his legs, Alec snorted. Only Tavish would say something so absurd. "I just met the lass. She is not bound to pick up and travel across the ocean to a place she is not verra familiar with." Alec felt a shadow over him. It was a shadow of authority with a hand on it's hip. The shadow definitely belonged to someone that was in the fifth of six stages of mad. Looking up shyly, he hoped that the look of complete innocence on his face would make the owner of that shadow a little less angry. However, as he saw a cross looking woman in a Sheriff's uniform staring down at him his hopes were dashed. Big sunglasses covered her eyes. Alec could feel the air of hostility aimed his way. It was like the summer heat steaming off of the pavement in Arizona from that time that his commanding officer had forced him to go to that international training event. They spent a half hour seeing how many eggs they could cook in the heat alone.

The woman's demeanor said it all as she changed her stance. Removing her hand from her hip she leaned back, placing all her weight on her left leg. Slowly she crossed her arms over her chest. With one foot slightly placed in front of the other and one eyebrow raised, he could tell this woman feared no one and no thing. The gun on her hip was within reach. The light reflected off of the star on her uniform. She was dangerous and she knew it.

Trouble. He was in big trouble. With a whispered confession directed at his brother he said, "Tavish, I think the magistrate's come to take me to jail."

"Good luck, Alec, I hear the Americans only let you make one call before they close the iron gates."

Really? That seemed kind of harsh. What if no one answered? Did you get to call again later on or was that it? "Then I better not call ye, eh?" The laughter of his brother was the only response he got as he hung up the phone. He swallowed his apprehension. Maybe he was just sitting in the wrong waiting area. At least he could hope that was what she wanted to yell at him about. "Is there anythin' I can do for ye, lass?"

The Sheriff uncrossed her arms from over her chest. The hand went back to the hip, the hip with the gun attached to it. Her fingers splayed as if she itched to pull it. Her left hand was stretched out in his direction. A long thin finger pointed at him, "You can start by explaining why you were driving a hundred and ten in a forty mile an hour zone. Then you can end by explaining why you brought in a beat up woman. You might even get a chance to finish with a plea as to why I shouldn't cart you off to jail, before I toss you on your stomach. That's if you're lucky. I don't think you're going to be lucky though."

This was not going to end well. Nancy should never have convinced him to come here to be free of his pain. If he had just stayed in Ullapool none of this would have happened. "I was tryin' to get the lass to help as quick I could. Someone put the fear in her eyes and when I went to see what it was about the lass was lyin' in a pile. There was broken glass 'round her and it irked me somethin' terrible. Someone hurt my lass…" Alec stopped as he realized he said his lass. Thinking about it he realized it was not the only time he had referred to her as such either. He wondered why he was declaring that this woman he had only known for two days was his. What exactly did that mean?

"Well, Mister, if that's the case then you'll kindly show me some identification and we can get this whole matter cleared up in no time."

"Yer determined to take me to jail."

"Quite possibly."

At least she was honest. Alec stood and slowly pulled out his wallet. The old black leather felt smooth with a familiarity of the years of daily touch it had received. His fingers knew it, like he knew his own skin. It had been a gift from his mother when he had started his first job, something to hold all the money he would earn. His first dollar still resided within it, all these years later. He handed her his international driver's license and sat back down. She glared at it for a second before saying, "Alright, Alec MacDaniel, how do you know her and what is her name?"

Alec almost choked and wondered if he should give her the fiancée story like he had the nurse. He thought about it for a second and then decided he should. "Amy and I are going to be married."

Removing the dark sunglasses, she turned a look of malice on him. The sheriff's brown almond shaped eyes narrowed dangerously, "Mr. MacDaniel, I'm a pretty honest person. When someone's not honest with me it tends to piss me off. Especially if I've been honest with them. I'm going to give you one more chance because I'm afraid I don't believe that cockamamy story."

"An' why not?"

She handed him back his license. "Because if your Amy is Amy Killigan then she is married...to a cop killer." Alec felt his stomach roll as a thousand questions flew through his mind. The sheriff's face softened as she saw the genuine surprise and confusion on his face. "Mr.

MacDaniel, I don't know much about Amy Killigan, but I do know that she's been through a lot. In fact, she's been through quite a bit lately. We found a body late last night and believed it to be a suspect we've been looking for. The identification was made from a wallet found on the victim, but now we know that the wallet wasn't the victim's. We tried to confirm it with fingerprints this morning. Unfortunately, it was a bit of a surprise when the results came back. They came back a lot faster than they should have. The reason for this is that we already had them on file. You see we found out the body is actually a cop. One that use to be one of my deputies. He was let go because of a lack of protecting the peace, a lack of protecting the people that he swore to protect. You see, I don't like my deputies failing the people of New Hope. I take that as a personal affront. That's exactly what he did. Haven't seen him in a few months, so no one questioned who the body belonged to until we got the printout.

"I tried to call Mrs. Killigan back to warn her, but when I received no answer at her work or home I went to personally investigate. My guys had already failed her once. Unfortunately, I'm still learning how bad we failed her. Eventually maybe we can make it right…"

She looked so sad that Alec wondered just what Amy had been through.

"Imagine my surprise though, when a black Porsche goes speeding past me. I sent some of my guys to check out her place while I talked to the doctors here. Should have a report from my guys here any minute. Oh, I put a ticket on your windshield. You can pay it at City Hall."

Alec opened his mouth to ask one of the many questions floating around in his mind, but shut it as the nurse from earlier walked towards him. "Sir, the doctors are finished patching her up and Dr. Michaels will be out in a second to talk to you." Alec nodded his thanks before she walked away.

"Mr. MacDaniel, I don't think I introduced myself, but I'm Sergeant in Charge Leann Newcastle. Mrs. Killigan has been in hiding for some time now from what I gather through police reports here in New Hope and in San Diego. It's almost a sure bet that her husband did this to her and to be honest we may not be able to catch him before he strikes again. He's killed a DEA Agent and an ex-deputy so far. I'm afraid there's no telling how many more he'll kill to get to her." Leann's phone rang and she excused herself to talk to her deputy.

He hung his head in shame. How could such a pixie thing deal with this? If there was one thing he could do for her it was offer her safety. In Ullapool, his family had been doing such for centuries. In fact, his father had been the one that protected his mother, that was how they met. Alec had done it once upon a time too. It had gotten Morvena killed, but maybe… Maybe he could save someone else, perhaps that would help ease some of the guilt he felt at losing Morvena. He made a vow he would protect Amy Killigan from any further harm. This woman that had only been a source of irritation at first meeting had some how struck that protective cord in him. He knew just the way to ensure her safety too. He would deal with her anger later and he was sure there would be a lot of it. He pulled his cell phone back out and dialed his mother. A young voice answered, "Mac-Daniel's Inn, how may I help ye?"

"Alison?"

"Alec?"

"What are ye doin' answerin' the phone? I thought the chef stayed in the kitchen?"

"And I thought the highlanders stayed in the highlands. Could have fooled me, Alec MacDaniel. 'Sides, I'm 'bout to leave on a short holiday." He could hear the smile in her voice.

"Aye, I probably should have stayed at home." If he had what would have happened to Amy? The very thought that she could still be lying on the floor, dying, made his throat close. Clearing it he whispered, "Is Mum nearby?"

"Aye, she's leanin' towards the phone, tryin' to catch every word she can." He heard a screech of laughter as his mother chased Alison away from the phone.

"Och, lad of mine, what is this I'm hearin' from Tavish about my oldest bein' locked away by the magistrate? Ye of all my children should ken better!" Love, fear, and reproach laced her voice. His mother was the only woman he knew that could put forth such conflicting emotions in just a few words. Sheena MacDaniel could slice you from head to toe while offering you a hot beverage to warm your soul.

"Not now, Mum, I need to bring a guest home. Can the lass have a room at the Inn for a few weeks?"

"Alec, dear son of mine, what have ye gotten into?" Her voice was filled with concern, making Alec's chest ache.

More than she could possibly imagine. He may no longer work for the Yard, but he could certainly still find trouble it seemed. "Please, Mum, let her have a room for a while?"

"Aye, the lass can stay for as long as she needs. When will ye be here?"

Alec sighed in relief. "As soon as the doctor let's the lass leave we'll be on our way." He looked up as the doctor came walking to him. "I've got to go, Mum, love ye and see ye soon." Without waiting for her to respond he hung up the phone. It was better that way. She would skewer him when he returned home, but for now he could deal with the problem at hand. As he stood he realized there were others he had to convince of his plan. One person might even give him trouble.

The doctor tilted his head and looked Alec up and down. "Are you the fiancée?" Alec nodded and the doctor held out his hand, "I'm Dr. Michaels." As Alec shook it he was aware of the Sheriff coming to stand beside him. "We found Ms. Killigan's wallet in her back pocket and were able to get medical information from her Veterans ID. We did this in order to look for allergy information and medical conditions before we treated her. It's standard policy here. We also have to notify the closest VA that she's here."

Veterans ID? The only Veterans he knew of were those that fought in wars. Was she... Had she been a soldier? So many layers to this young woman. It seemed that no one had ever been able to get through them all because Lilly had neglected to mention this to him when she was so busy regaling all of her benefits.

"Now, in regards to her injuries, she has a minor concussion from blunt force trauma to the temporal region." The doctor pointed to just above his left ear. "We gave her three stitches to close the wound. They need to stay dry for twenty-four hours and since they're dissolvable she will not have to worry about having them removed. She's also got several scrapes from glass and we've treated those. However, her ribcage is already starting to bruise. It looks like someone stomped on her side. If that is the case, then over the next few days bruising in the form of shoe prints may be visible. We wanted to make sure the ribs weren't broken, so we did some x-rays." The doctor went quiet, his brown eyes assessing Alec, as if determining his very worth.

"What tis it?" The silence was worrisome. There was so much that this man was not saying. The look said it all though. They had found something, something this man did not condone. They had found something that made him angry, angry to his very core.

"How long have you two been together?"

Should he tell the truth? Or just stick as close to the truth as possible? "Not verra long. A bit of a whirlwind if ye must know. Still learning each other's secrets at this stage."

"Have you ever hit her?"

"What?" The question shocked him. He would never hit a woman. In fact, even when Morvena had been raging at him he had never so much as raised his voice at her, much less a hand.

"Are you left handed?"

"No, my right tis my dominant hand. What tis this about?"

The doctor nodded, "The x-rays showed numerous damage along the first four ribs on her right side. Some are a few years old, but there's a few that are a little more recent. Six months if I had to guess. Her clavicle, 6th rib, and scapula show numerous fractures. I'd be amazed if she does not develop arthritis in those bones before she's in her late thirties."

Dear God. What on Earth had she survived? Was this what she had been running from for so long? Was this why she acted so prickly? Even though they had not been around each other much, he could imagine that a thorny cactus was easier to handle than her. If this was her past though, he could see why. Such a tiny woman to have been dealt such a crummy hand.

"She was very lucky that none of the ribs were broken this time, but one was cracked and could break all the way through if she's not careful. She should be awake here soon, but we want to keep her for a bit, just for observation. Probably just overnight. After we have determined that everything looks good you should be able to take her home. When you are ready to see her let Nurse Benson over at the intake desk know and she'll take you up to your fiancée. We're going to be moving her up to the second floor. They will monitor her from there. Do you have any questions for me?"

Alec let out a deep sigh of relief and thanked the doctor. He smiled brightly knowing that she would be released soon. The sooner the better as far as he was concerned, although, he needed time to think of a plan to get her to Ullapool. He felt his smile waver. Would she even agree to go?

Of course she would. What woman would turn down a chance to go to Scotland? Satisfied that everything would turn out well the smile returned full force. Turning back to the seat he had vacated when the doctor arrived, he noticed the Sheriff standing not too far away. His smile vanished when he saw her face. It was the same look his mother had when he was preparing for his wedding. It was the look of a woman determining whether or not to say something she knew would not go over well. "Is somethin' the matter?"

"Mr. MacDaniel…"

"Tis alright. Just say it. I promise everything will be just fine."

She snorted, "Yeah, just fine. Of course it will be. Because we live in a fantasy world where everything always turns out alright…"

He raised an eyebrow. Even in the short time since he had met her he could tell that she did not often use sarcasm. It did not suit her. While it was true that he tended to view the world through rose colored glasses, despite his losses, he knew that there was evil in the world. His job had taught him that. Watching her take a deep breath, he knew that whatever she was about to say would change his life. He was not yet sure how it would change it, only that it would.

"My deputy said the place had been trashed badly. He also said there's graffiti on the walls. It was her husband alright and he just got a new target in his sights..."

"Who?" Alec was not really sure he wanted to know the answer to that question, but felt he had to ask it anyways.

"You..."

CHAPTER 9

ALEC SPOKE WITH THE SHERIFF about options just down the hall from Amy's room on the second floor. There was not much they could do while they waited for her to wake up. The doctor said it might take a while, but that when she woke she should be fine. The doctor was wrong in that. There was no way a woman would be fine after dealing with such atrocities perpetrated by someone she had once loved. There was no way a man would either. Alec knew that from the things he had seen while on the job.

The doctor was deluded. Or crazy. Alec preferred to think he was crazy — batshit crazy, with a side of never-gonna-happen.

The Sheriff turned sharply, her mouth in a tight line. "Alec, I don't think you understand how dangerous this guy is. Matthew Killigan is a murderer. I know you're just here for a respite, but you need to leave. Now."

As he leaned back against the wall he shrugged. "I will nae." The wall felt solid beneath his back. It gave him the sense that he could fight Amy's demons for her. Strength seemed to flow from it into him. It had been so long since he had such a purpose in life, so long since Morvena.

"Look, this guy has killed way too many people. I can see why the Navy dishonorably discharged him. Military guys are supposed to be protectors, not murderers. This guy has been trained to be an assassin. By the government, of all people! Do you know what that means!?!"

He shrugged. It honestly did not matter what it meant. He was not going anywhere. There was a purpose here. He could finally make it up to Morvena by protecting Amy.

"There's no hope for you here. Don't you get that? Nothing in this world can help you here."

"Sheriff, in a place called New Hope, why would ye say there tis no hope?" He smiled sadly at her. "There tis always hope. No matter how small, tis still there." He looked back towards the tile floor. That was something that he had forgotten along the way. "I will return home when I decide to. Amy needs someone to help her. Why has no one helped the lass before now?"

Sighing the Sheriff leaned against the wall. Her shoulders fell and a deep weariness came over her, telling Alec everything he needed to know. "We always thought she was hiding something when her brother was murdered. It was supposedly a shooting gone wrong kind of thing. I always thought there was something she wasn't saying though. Something that she was afraid to say. Then we got the results back... it wasn't who we thought it was. Turns out that the body we recently discovered was the deputy that we believed was responsible for shooting her brother, Finn. Supposedly he was the first on the scene. He had always denied it, but he had a personal gun on him at the time. It wasn't registered to him, but it was a match to some other slugs we found on site. His issued gun was fired at the scene too. A slug was pulled out of the ground underneath her brother. It was believed to be the shot that killed him.

"The case was sort of open and shut at that point. She refused to talk and he claimed innocence." Alec watched as her shoulders fell. It seemed that the case had affected her deeply. "The evidence spoke too highly against him, so we put him on suspension pending an investigation. He didn't take it well… As far as I was concerned even if he didn't kill Finn Lee, he was sure as hell guilty of not protecting him. I won't have that kind of cowardly bullshit going on with my deputies." The sadness seemed to disappear and a calm anger took its place. "If he wouldn't tell the whole truth and try to fix it the best he could, then he was a coward. Simple as that. My deputies failed Amy Killigan before. Now Matthew Killigan could be anywhere waiting for her. She needs to go into protective custody. I don't want us to be the reason that she's harmed yet again."

She had been through so much. So many people had hurt her. Did she not have anyone that she could turn to? No one that would stand up for her? No one that would help her? What would her future be like if no one helped her now? Would she even have a future? What sadness she must feel at not knowing such a thing…

Turning away from the Sheriff he saw a male nurse come out of Amy's room. The man wore a white coat, a surgical mask, and gloves. Something was… off… about him. As he walked down the hall he stopped at the trash can and tossed a syringe in it.

Alec's breath caught. That was not standard practice. He had seen the sharps containers. There was even one in Amy's room…

Taking off at a full out run he heard the blaring sirens from Amy's monitors. He gave chase, but the man had already disappeared down the hall. Turning back he hoped he was wrong, but as he came to Amy's room he saw that her face was turning blue. Her lips were puffy. Her chest was still. He had gotten to her! Right under their noses, the bastard had gotten to her!

Several people pushed past him into the room, bumping into him as they went. So still. She was so still.

A nurse pushed him back. "Sir, go. We need to be able to work." How could he leave when he could not even move? It was his fault. He failed her. Just like he failed Morvena. "In order to save her we need you to stay out here." Then the door was closed in his face.

The door closing seemed to signify his failure. He had wondered why no one had protected her. Now, he had his answer. Even he had failed to protect her, failing her almost right away. Her life hung in the balance because he had not been paying attention. His breath caught. His throat felt clogged with emotion. It was as if the world had just shut down. Waiting to spin again felt like an eternity was passing. Universes were being born, life times were being lived. Yet, time stood still for him — frozen while everyone else lived on.

If only she would breathe for them.

Reaching out he put a hand on the door that served as a barrier. The cold metal was a match for how his insides felt — cold and hard, yet unbending to his will. Had he truly failed her too? So many wrongs done to her over her life, yet she had smiled. A beautiful smile too, as radiant as the sun on a beautiful Scottish summer day. Her soul as sweet as the heather swaying in the breeze. Despite everything done to her, she was still beautiful.

His stomach clenched as he longed to see her smile again, even if just for a moment, just one blissful moment.

He would not bend until he righted this wrong, even if

he was just a bystander. Maybe it was in his blood. Maybe it was just the way he was raised. Maybe it was still the investigator in him. Who knew. The one thing he did know, with every fiber of his being, was she deserved better though. She deserved better from everyone. It was time she had a protector. "I will protect ye, Amy Killigan. I swear that no one shall harm ye from this moment on, as long as there is breath left in this body."

He felt the Sheriff stepping up behind him. As she put her hand on his shoulder he turned towards her. Once he made a decision nothing would deter him from it, not even a Sheriff. Tapping into what he had been taught as a child, his heritage, he felt strength, strength in the knowledge that he had the ability to do what needed to be done. He had the knowledge from years of training to be able to protect Amy, he just needed to get her to a place where nothing else could interfere - or distract him. Allowing the anger he felt to boil over slightly, he glared at the Sheriff. "No one shall harm the lass ever again."

He let her steer him away from the door, preparing himself for anything she might say as she took a deep breath. It was almost as if she was steeling herself to accept any wrath he might toss her way. If she planned on stopping him there would be plenty of it too. He would move Heaven and Earth to get his way. Never again would he fail Amy, no matter how long it took.

"Alec, you must understand that the doctors will do their best to save her. You must also understand that choices have to be made. She needs to go into protective custody, but I'm not sure how much good it will do her. You see... From what I've learned, there's history here. Serious history.

"I doubt any of his Navy comrades will help him. Navy

tends to frown on this kind of stuff and once they found out he was doing drugs they dishonorably discharged him through Court Martial. That doesn't mean that he won't find someone to help him get to her though. She needs to get out of here. She needs to go somewhere safe."

Pursing his lips, he knew the perfect place for her, a place were she would find the sanctuary she so desperately needed. "I will arrange it. Amy will be safe with me. No lass deserves this." Especially not his lass. He would protect her no matter what and he knew just the guys to help. In his world, family could always be counted on, especially his family.

"What makes you think that you can protect her? You saw that he got to her, even with us standing right here."

"I'm a Scotland Yard Investigator." It was true too. He may be on leave… for an undetermined amount of time, he might even be a little rusty, but it was time. It was time for him to do the job that he ran from. No one else could protect her. Maybe he could. He had to at least try. There was no way he could stand aside and watch someone else be harmed just because he was lacking. Alec just had to pretend that the very thought of holding a gun again didn't make his stomach curdle, his palms sweat, or the ground move beneath his feet. If he could get past that then perhaps he could save Amy, and maybe Morvena's spirit would leave him alone.

CHAPTER 10

A S THE DOOR BEGAN TO open, Alec looked up from where he was curled up against the wall. His arms loosened from where they were circled protectively around his knees. An eternity had passed since the door had been closed in his face. Would they have good news? Pushing off the wall, he stood up and walked towards the nurse that had shut the door in his face. Several nurses and doctors walked out of the room. "Sir, the doctor would like to speak with you before you enter."

Fear gripped him. A cold sensation passed throughout his stomach. Was she alive? Had they lost the battle to save her? Everything was an unknown. At least as an unknown the news was not definitively bad, even though unknowns could be dangerous. Like the deep blue sea, danger lurked, waiting to gobble him up if he so much as moved. Maybe that was why he had pulled back from everyone after Morvena, so he would never fall into that deep abyss again.

The nurse quickly waved her hands. "Don't worry, she's going to be fine. He just needs to talk to you first, so please wait here." Her smile was probably meant to reassure him, but the reassurances were useless. Until he knew Amy was safe, everything was useless.

The wait for the doctor to exit seemed like an eternity. Whole lives were lived in the five minute timespan that it took for the doctor to exit the room. A quick look behind the doctor, as he made his exit, into the room told Alec that a nurse remained with Amy. As the doctor close the door behind him Alec's stomach clenched. The look upon his face was a sad one. "Amy... the lass..."

The doctor held up his hands, "She's going to be just fine. We've got her breathing on her own again." Dear Lord. How long had she quit breathing for? "She is, however, going to sleep for a bit longer." As the doctor motioned to the opposite wall, Alec allowed him to lead him away from the door back across the hall. The lights were dark to reflect the late hour. The silence in the hallway was peaceful yet disturbing at the same time — peaceful because it meant that Amy was safe, for the time being.

They needed to know. "There was a man..."

The doctor nodded, "He injected something into her I.V.. It looks like she had an allergic reaction to it, but it's looking like there might be something else that was mixed with it. We're going to run some blood tests to try to determine what it is exactly, but we've injected her with a dose of Epinephrine and a high dose of Benadryl. We also noticed signs of drug overdose, so we're treating that as well. This seems to have stabilized her, but the nurse is going to stay with her for a while just to keep an eye on her."

Drug overdose? At least they were going to have someone with her. That was a plus. It was not really necessary though because he had no plans to leave her again. "What drug?"

"Once we know the medicine is working to combat

what he used then we'll focus more on other avenues. The main thing to keep in mind is that he could have injected her with anything. I'm going to be honest with you. It's highly unlikely, but it's possible that the drug could have long term consequences. It's just a waiting game right now."

"When will ye know what drug the bastard used?" Rage filled him. When they caught Matthew there was going to be hell to pay. Ticking off the number of body parts he could rip from the bastard's body quelled the rage enough to listen to the doctor.

As he shifted from one foot to the other, the doctor replied, "It's too soon to tell. The lab has to break it down. Could be fast if it's a well known one, but if it's homemade then it could be a day. There's just no telling at this time how long it will take. I wish there was an easier way to handle this, but this is a first for us." With a deep sigh he exclaimed, "I'm sorry. If we had known we would have asked security to look out for her. I'll see if I can push the lab to work quickly on the breakdown. I'll get them to start first with her known allergies. Maybe it'll be simple…"

"It's anything but simple when he tried to murder her." Alec turned towards the voice of the Sheriff. Her eyes were focused, her hand on her gun as she walked down the hallway. There was a fire in her step. Slow and burning, but it was there. Her shoulders were taunt, ready for action. She was focused, not on any one thing but on everything. The Sheriff was ready for the monsters that could jump out at her. Unfortunately, no one knew where the monsters were. "Just finished reviewing the tapes with your security guys. By the way, doc, your security cameras are a joke. A two year old could hack them with a toy phone."

The doctor looked a little exasperated, "Leann, I told you already. They are NOT my guys. I do not have GUYS." It was like they forgot he was there. "I know they could use a bit of training, but they're what we have to work with right now. Unfortunately, our budget is a little strained at the moment."

"Doc, I told you. It's Sheriff when I'm working." She crossed her arms over her chest. The self protective movement was not lost on Alec. They knew each other alright. It was a very personal type of knowledge too if the way she looked away from the doctor was anything to go by. They were acting like children. There's only one thing that could make adults act like that.

"You weren't working last night." Yep, they were intimate with each other.

Her entire head rapidly cut towards the doctor and Alec took a step back. It was amazing that she did not have whiplash from it. "Logan, this is not the time nor the place." The icy tone of her words combined with her eyes burned gave Alec the impression that she could be deadly when it warranted it. Maybe even deadly when it did not warrant it. It seemed that she had a bit of a temper. "There's more important things to discuss right now."

"Things that are more important than budgets, grudges, and names."

"Please, what did ye learn?" Alec prayed that the conversation would go back towards his lass. He needed to know for sure that she would be safe, that no further harm would be caused by the drugs. It was as if the world had gone mad. Nothing was right until he knew she was safe. Such an unusual thing too, knowing that his world depended upon the safety of someone else. It was not something he was prepared to consider just yet.

For now, he would prefer to believe that he felt this way simply because he had failed her too. Once he corrected that wrong then things would return to normal. He would no longer feel as if his world depended upon her safety. The world needed to return to normal. This was too messy. Messy was hard. He could not handle messy. Yes, the world had to be returned to normal. Only then would things make sense again.

With one last glare in the doctor's direction the Sheriff continued, "The cameras made it a little hard to tell, but I'm almost positive that it's Matthew Killigan. I can't believe he was able to get to her here."

A nurse entered the hallway. "Pardon me. Doctor," she held up a piece of paper. "The lab sent this for you. Jackson called the nurses station and said you'd want to see it right away." The doctor turned towards her and walked away. That piece of paper was important, he was sure of it. Why could they not just say things that were important and be done with it? Everything was like a secret with doctors, a secret that they were determined would never go over well with the ones involved so it had to be hidden.

Alec turned back to the wall. This was not the time to let his anger out. He had spent so long burying it after her death. The smells, sights, and sounds would make him go crazy if he let them. Reigning in his temper was the most important thing for him to do. Focus on the problem, not the past. Focus on success, not failure.

More importantly, who was this man that kept hurting her but never got caught? Wasn't there anyone that could help her? "Sheriff, I need to know everything about this bastard that ye can share."

"I'll have one of my deputies bring a copy of the file from my office. I'm not sure what good it'll do. Can't hurt though."

After a few minutes the doctor walked back to Alec and the Sheriff. "The good news is that the drug she was injected with has been matched. Did the ER staff tell you that she has an allergy to Codeine?" Alec nodded. "Well, it looks like that's what he injected her with." The doctor paused and gave the Sheriff a look. It was a questioning look. Alec saw her shake her head from the corner of his eye before the doctor continued. What were they keeping from him? "This means a couple different things; however, the good news is Epi and Benadryl should do the trick. Once the interaction fades a bit she should wake up."

"Will she have any problems from it?"

"I honestly don't think there will be any side effects other than she'll be sleepy. She probably won't even feel all the pain she should be in."

CHAPTER 11

THE SMELL OF ANTISEPTIC DRIFTED in her dreams. Sterile. Soft and sterile, were her first thoughts. The strong invasive smell could serve as a wake up call to the dead. There was no way to hide from it once it was noticed. Unfortunately.

As awareness came, the softness of the bed came with it. It was like a water bed, moving of it's own accord, enveloping one in comfort, but there was no feeling of water within it. Amy shifted in the bed and yawned sleepily. Her body ached. In fact, the list of places that did not hurt was shorter than the list of places that did. She could feel the bruises that were making themselves known. In an effort to pretend that they did not exist, she rolled onto her side to curl up into a fetal position while burying her head beneath the blanket.

The plan was no longer feasible. Matthew knew where she was. There was no way it could work now. Heck, it was a wonder she was alive. If she was actually alive. Maybe they had warm soft beds in Heaven. Maybe you could feel your bruises there too. Maybe you were sup-posed to feel your bruises there.

A small chuckle made her go completely still. Maybe

she was actually in Hell… that would probably be why the bruises hurt so much. A hand reached out and lifted the blanket off of her head. Oh God! Was it Matthew? Was he still there? Was he trying to trick her into feeling complacent before he murdered her? There was only one way to find out. Slowly opening her eyes she looked up into Alec's ice blue eyes. Relief momentarily flooded her. "Uh… hi?"

Alec smiled brightly at her. "Lass, are ye attemptin' to smother yerself?"

As his tongue reached out just a bit to moisten his lip, she bet he could not help but think how sexy she looked with her curls splayed out on the sheets. He probably wondered if they would look the same splayed out on his pillow. The look in his eyes told her so. The color changed just a bit and his irises widened just enough to say he was attracted to her. Heck, her sleepy attitude probably made him wonder if she was the same when sated. From what she knew of guys, most would wonder that if they were looking at a woman the way Alec was looking at her.

In an effort to close down on the train of thought and his possible train of thought, she closed her eyes. Playfully she swatted at his hand while mumbling. "Sleepy, go away." Alec caught her hand and gently held it. Warning bells went off in her head. They were slightly muted from slumber, but they were the kind of warning bells that caused a person to stop whatever they were doing. They were the kind of warning bells that made one pay rapt attention. They warned of life changing danger.

This had to be stopped now. It could not be allowed to progress. No more stalkers were wanted by this woman. It was hard enough dealing with the one she had. Her body went still. Opening her eyes again, she took a slow

breath and glared at him. Just because he was attracted
to her did not mean he could just do that. It did not
mean he could take such liberties with her. "What do
you want?"

"Lass, we need to talk. The sheriff here wants to ask
ye some questions." She looked over and saw a woman
in a Sheriff's uniform standing near the doorway. "She
promises to ask quickly." Amy made a face at her before
glaring at Alec. His face was red, indicating barely suppressed the laughter threatening to come out. He could
just take his laughter and shove it up his... *Be nice, Ames,*
she reminded herself. It would not do her any good to
get worked up. Maybe if they thought everything was
fine they would leave her alone.

A sarcastic frown marred her face. "Alright, fine, ask
away, but I'm not moving. I'm comfortable where I'm
at." She barely noticed that Alec, sitting in the chair
against the wall directly beside the bed, was caressing
her hair. Or at least she would have if his soft hands were
not so surprisingly gentle while they lightly ran over her
tresses, so different from the last time a man touched her.
This brought butterflies to her stomach, if not chills to
her soul.

"Amy, we spoke on the phone yesterday morning, I'm
Leann Newcastle."

Relief flooded her. A familiar name, thank goodness.
"The sheriff, yeah I know. Wait…" It couldn't be. Could
it? "Yesterday morning…?" How long had she been out?
What had Matthew done to her? Oh God, had he… had
he hurt her like before? Embarrassment, fear, and shame
filled her. Damn him for making her feel this way again.
Averting her eyes to the wall seemed safer than looking
at either Alec or the Sheriff.

"Yes, ma'am. You've been out for almost a full twenty-four hours. There were some complications. Well, Um, first I've got some bad news. Do you remember me talking about the suspect? That I thought we had found him?"

"It wasn't him was it?" They were finally beginning to get it. Finally beginning to understand that things were more complex than they seemed. Could they understand it all though? Or would they condemn her for the secrets she had?

"How did you know that?"

Some things were better left unsaid. "Matthew, he didn't kill Jerry." Her voice broke, "Jerry helped him. The bastard paid him five thousand to bring me to him. Jerry admitted it. He was in the backseat of my jeep. Said he was supposed to bring me to Matthew." Alec's hand stilled for a few seconds before he continued his ministrations. Yes, there were secrets that she needed to keep. Telling them about Jerry was not going to harm her. It might even help them understand why the deputy acted the way he had.

"You're right. That wasn't the suspect that we found. It was the cop that wrote your brother the ticket. One of my deputies found a gun on your premises and ballistics matched the slug from Officer Tanner to that nine millimeter. We pulled some fingerprints off of it and they matched Matthew Killigan. I've always known that there was more going on than anyone said. I wish you would trust me enough to tell me."

If only she could trust. Unfortunately, her trust meter was broken and had been for a number of years now. Amy sighed, "I told them after he first started doing drugs that he was going to kill somebody outside of his line of work, but they didn't believe me." Amy felt completely relaxed under Alec's ministrations. "So what's the plan from here? Did you guys catch him or what?"

Leann shifted to her other foot nervously. "Well, that's where your buddy, Alec, comes in. I actually think he's got a great plan."

Why was he even here? What plan could he possibly have that she had not considered? Amy frowned. "What's this great plan?"

Alec's hand froze for a second before he sighed deeply. Something was wrong. What in the world could they have in store for her? It was as if he was contemplating his options before he decided to throw all his chips in, "I made arrangements for ye to return with me to Scotland here in a few hours."

Amy froze as she digested what he had said. "I'm sorry, do what?" If she heard him correctly then a man which she did not know, at all, had just made arrangements for her to flee to Scotland with him. "I think I got hit on the head harder than I thought. Or I really did die, and I just haven't adjusted to the concept yet." Who was he to think he could do such a thing?

Alec frowned. "Lass, ye dinnae die. Och, I am not that bad a lad."

"Sheriff, can you arrest him for lying?" That would be one way to get everyone off her back.

"Call me Leann." Great, now she's trying to establish a rappore. The fun would apparently never end as Leann smiled. "Amy, it's a good plan. Killigan's not going to look for you in a different country or if he tries to he'll get picked up the minute he gets off the plane. It will give us a chance to wait for him to slip up. If you're here we won't be able to do that." Leann looked away and mumbled, "Besides I already had one of my female deputies pack for you."

"What?" Amy could scarcely believe what she was

hearing. Everyone in the small town of New Hope was plotting against her, she was sure of it. "You had someone go through my stuff and pack it for me to go to another country with some stranger before you even talked with me about it?" It seemed like a violation of privacy to have someone you did not know going through your stuff. She would probably justify it by safety or something. At least they had not found her gun. Someone would have said something about it already if they had.

Leann put her hands on her hips, "I even had your ridiculously hyper mutt put in a crate for you. He'll be in baggage claim when you get there. That dog was a little upset when we found him hog tied in your bedroom, but he seems to have forgotten about it now. Thank goodness he's had all of his shots and could be certified. I didn't even know that whole process existed." The look on her face left no room for argument and Amy felt the world press in on her once again. Eventually maybe she could run her life without fear. Maybe she could actually live again.

"I don't have a choice do I?"

"Afraid not."

Shifting her stance just a bit gave her away. Matthew had done something else. Something bad. Something the Sheriff did not want to reveal. Had he branched out? Had he told them what he had done to her? Poised on pins and needles, she had to know! "What did he do? Please, just tell me."

"Hon, I don't know how to tell you this, but someone tried to kill you with codeine after you were brought in." She took a deep breath. "It seems that I can't protect you here in New Hope. I honestly don't think he'll be looking for you in another country. I've looked up this guy," she inclined her head towards Alec, "and he seems to be pretty trustworthy. I really think it's for the best. I assure you that I don't say that lightly. My guys messed up and you're paying the price. I think this might be the only way to help you. Just stick to the fiancé story and you'll be fine."

It was a lost cause, didn't matter if she put up a fight. Their decisions were made. Nothing she could do to change it. There were just some things in life that were not worth fighting or fighting about. Instead she nodded her agreement. It was much easier just to go back to sleep. It was easy too, with the way Alec was caressing her hair. Such gentle hands he had.

It would be nice to follow her dreams of seeing Scotland before Matthew killed her. At least then she could be proud of something she had done. Everything else in her life had turned out rather harshly. Maybe Alec could protect her. Maybe he could even save her. Or maybe he would fail. No one else was interested enough to even try. Might as well let him give it a go. As her breathing began to even out she mumbled, "Fiancé story?"

CHAPTER 12

AS AMY AND ALEC GOT off the plane he watched her face. Her eyes were wide and she looked slightly skittish. It was possible that she wondered what on Earth she had done. She was probably fully prepared to blame the knock to her head for her agreeing to this ridiculous scheme, but who knew for sure. Maybe she honestly was not too sure if it was that alone. He had taken a gamble at the hospital by proposing bringing her home to Scotland. He was still amazed that she agreed to it. He had a feeling that his hands on her hair had played a major part in getting her to agree to it. Sometimes you just had to play dirty though.

Alec placed one hand on the small of her back and steered her off the plane. He thought he felt her shiver under his touch, but dismissed it. He knew his brother Rory would be waiting for them while the rest would be at the Inn. Ian was coming a few days earlier due to the excitement, but it was still two more days before he would be there. His family would be together again. Well, mostly together again.

He smiled thinking about how understanding Nancy had been when he had cancelled the rest of his stay. She had actually winked at him and told him to be quick about the wooing. He could not ask for a better friend sometimes. He smiled secretively as he thought about it.

It would be fantastic to woo Amy; however, his first duty was to protect her. He also sensed it would be some time before Amy was ready to be wooed. The wide-eyed woman in front of him would probably not even realize he was trying unless it was something akin to lighting off fireworks, shouting it off rooftops, etc. Maybe then she would stand back and realize that she was sexy. Even her curiosity was sexy. On the flight over he had told her all about his family. Well, except for Danny. It was still so hard to speak of him. He had also neglected to mention Morvena. People looked at him differently when they realized that he was a widower. Sometimes it was best just to ignore that he had ever been married. Sometimes it was safer.

Speaking about his brother was just hard. At least with Morvena he knew she was dead. No one knew for sure whether Danny was or not. He had been missing for months. One day there was a knock at the door, and they were just supposed to accept that the military was looking for him. Maybe they were, but it was doubtful that they would find him. There were so many places in the Middle East that he could be, so many things that could have happened…

Drawing himself back to the current problem at hand Alec took a deep breath. Amy needed him. He would not fail her again. "Amy, Rory will be waiting by the baggage claim. He might seem a bit scary to ye, but dinnae fash yerself. He will be good to ye. I promise on my life." His brothers had already sworn that they would help protect her. That was the only assurances that he needed in order to know that she would be safe with his kin. Let the bastard come find her. They would be ready and waiting for him.

Steering her away from the people departing the flight with them, he watched as she took in the sights. It was home to him, but he remembered his first flight to the states. Everything was new and exciting. Like a child he had played with the trinkets in the shops in the airports while waiting for his next flight. He had bought a few. He had even stood amongst the people and watched them as they ran from place to place with children in tow, dragging small suitcases with wheels, or even carrying large paper cups filled with coffee. This airport was smaller than the one had stood in ages ago; however, she looked around with the same wonder he had. It left a strange feeling within him, one of satisfaction

His hands were so gentle at her back, yet she could feel the strength in them. She seriously doubted that she could think when those hands were touching her. Maybe that would explain her going along with this crazy fiancé plan. If it didn't then she needed to have her head examined. Did Alec have any idea of how dangerous Matthew could be? He had murdered a DEA Agent, a Sheriff's Deputy, and a cop. None of them had ever done anything wrong. Well, none of them other than the Deputy. He deserved to be punished, but he didn't deserve to die.

Sadness took over. People were walking all around her and Alec. Some had children, some had significant others, and others… they had whole lives that they were living — memories of good moments, and were on their way to do great things. She was simply running from a murderer… a murderer that wanted her dead because she knew his secret. She knew his trade routes…

"Are ye alright?"

"Yes, I was just thinking." He tilted his head at her and she knew the question he was bound to ask. "I was thinking that I shouldn't be here."

"Bollocks."

"What?"

"It means…"

"I know what it means." She stopped him. "I've just never heard anyone use it before." Grinning at him, she shook her head. The word struck her as odd, but hilarious. "I'm going to use that word one day, just because I can." She would too, when he least expected it.

CHAPTER 13

WHEN THEY GOT PAST THE gate Amy saw a tall man with dark black hair and sea green eyes waving to them. She vaguely remembered thinking Alec looked like a God when she had seen him and this guy reminded her of that. Where Alec walked like he was reserved and taking everything in this guy stalked like a predator. Amy felt a bit fearful and once again questioned her sanity, but her fears were calmed when the guy introduced himself. "Och, Alec, this is quite a bonnie lass, if I say so myself. Lass are ye sure ye want this old sod?"

She looked from Rory to Alec to get a feel of the tone and calmed when she saw Alec's grin. She stuck out her hand. "You must be Rory. I'm Amy."

Rory made a small face at the extended hand, but shook it anyways. "Normally we hug, but I think we'll make an exception for such a bonnie lass."

Amy quickly took her hand back and crossed her arms. She stepped closer to Alec as if seeking protection and Rory laughed. Alec smiled. "Well, let's make our way before mum has a stroke."

Rory was pushed forward as a guard went running by screaming into a walkie-talkie. "Will, get that hound from hell! He's coming up on yer side!"

Amy gasped. "They're talking about Rocky!"

Rory straightened himself. "The lass knows a hound from hell?"

Alec grinned. "Worse, the lass brought him with her."

She looked at Alec with fear in her eyes. "Do something or they're going to hurt him! I can't let anything happen to him too!"

"Will ye give me yer solemn vow not to hit me when ye meet the rest of my family?" She nodded and his grin grew. "I'll be right back." He walked over to a small food stand and bought a hot dog. He poured some ketchup on it and walked back. He looked at Amy with mirth in his eyes. "Now whistle for the hound." She did and a few seconds later a tan blur knocked Alec over to get to the hot dog.

The guards came running over panting for breath. "Who's mutt is this?" Amy shyly raised her hand and the guard glared at her. "Lass, ye can't be bringing in terrors to Inverness. That hound ate through his blasted crate and several pieces of luggage." Alec started laughing and the guard turned to him. "Well, I'll be, if it isn't Alec MacDaniel himself."

"Aye, MacDougall, it 'tis me. The last time I saw ye I was leaving for college, almost nine years ago." MacDougall stuck his hand out as an offering and Alec took it. As Alec stood, Rocky sat on his haunches and licked the ketchup from his chops. Amy grabbed him by the scruff of his neck to keep him in line. It was a loose hold that he could have easily gotten out of, but he seemed to understand it was not the time to run amuck.

MacDougall noticed Rory and heartily shook hands with him as well. "Rory, tis great to see ye too! How is my wee brother doing?"

Did everyone know everyone here? Was Scotland really that tiny? It seemed to be.

"Och. The lad is a unique one. We had to take his weapon away twice last week."

MacDougall laughed heartily and Alec leaned towards her. "Rory is the Constable for Ullapool. MacDougall's young brother is his new hire." Constable? Rory was a cop? Alec brought her home to a cop?

Her stomach flipped. Why had she agreed to this? Matthew was just going to kill him too. He would follow them. There was no way that he would let this go. If he had the chance to kill another cop? Well, he'd look at it like a child in a candy store — a challenge.

"Is this yer lass then?" Alec nodded and Amy stuck out her tongue at him. This caused MacDougall to laugh. "A right fiery one ye picked."

"Tell me 'bout it. The lass keeps claimin' I kidnapped her."

She frowned deeply. He had technically kidnapped her. There was no way she could have made a conscious decision after what had happened. Heroin. They had found heroin in her system. She had never done drugs before in her life and it broke her heart to know that they had been forced upon her. Something that she had been so proud of, was now no more. Now it was just something else on the list that Matthew had done.

"Dinnae tell her that's how us Scots get our bonnie brides did ye?" His eyes were full of mirth and Amy wanted to smack him for it. Alec looked at her with fire in his eyes causing her to wonder about her assessment of Rory as the predator. When Alec licked his lips that cinched it, she had been tricked. He had captured her hook, line, and sinker. Now, he was slowly dragging her into his predator's web for the rest of the way home.

Much like a spider trying to trap a fly, wrapping it up in its silken web saving it for later.

Amy had been a history major in college and Mac-Dougall was not just pulling her leg. Scots did have a habit of kidnapping their brides centuries ago. A part of her felt a tiny bit thrilled at the idea that Alec MacDaniel might just be trying the relive the tradition, a thrill that she thought she had long since buried deep within, in a locked box with the key tossed away, then covered it with layers of concrete and barbed wire.

"Alec," the sense of mirth disappeared from MacDougall's tone. "I was sorry to hear about Morvena. She was…"

"Not now," Alec whispered. His jaw was clenched so tightly. It was amazing that his teeth did not shatter under the pressure. His shoulders were hunched up. Pain, severe emotional pain laced his features.

MacDougall nodded at Alec. Who was Morvena and what happened to her? Why did the mention of her name cause Alec so much pain? The look on Alec's face mirrored one that she had seen in the mirror repeatedly. Every day for the last six months, in fact. It was a look of loss, one that he blamed himself for.

Did she really want to go anywhere with a man that seemed to be mourning the loss of someone he loved? Especially when Matthew could be anywhere? Why was Alec trying to protect her anyways? Was it because he felt guilty about this Morvena? Had he done something to her? Was that why he was trying to protect her?

CHAPTER 14

AN HOUR AND A HALF later they pulled into the driveway to the Inn in Ullapool. On the plane, Alec had explained how his family was well known. The Inn that they owned was one of many bed and breakfasts within the small town in the Highlands of Scotland, but this one was among the larger inns. It was close to the Falls of Mesach, making it perfect for tourists. They were just a short drive from town, but close enough to the falls to make it worthwhile. It provided a sense of peace and was perfect for newlyweds. The drive had been made in silence though. The only sound was the wind whooshing in from the partially opened window.

Alec jumped out and opened the back passenger door for her. She slowly got out, her ribs protesting loudly as she stood with shaky movements. Each breath and movement seemed to cause them to stretch and bend in ways that felt inhumane. The pain streaked from her sternum around to her spine. The pain made her feel weak. So weak. As if he noticed, Alec placed his hand on the small of her back to steady her. He took Rocky's leash in the other hand he stood close enough to look as if he was merely standing within a few inches of her. In reality it wasn't just the closeness that made her believe it was safe, it was that he was lending her his strength. His body and his very soul seemed to overshadow hers. While the action seemed almost natural on his part, it made her feel protected, protected in a way that she had not felt in so long. The touch made her yearn for more.

"Now, don't be afraid. My brothers are easy going and my mum and da' are the same."

Her feet felt like they had grown roots, sluggish and refusing to yield from their spot. "Dude, you're bringing home a girl that has a murderer after her and it's not just any murderer... it's someone she married. If your family doesn't lynch me on the spot then I might be inclined to believe that they're a bit more than easy going." How in the world had she kept the fear out of her voice?

The front door to the inn opened and a slim woman stepped out. Her hair was raven black with tinges of grey and her eyes ice blue. She had crinkles around her eyes from happiness and it just added to the effect. Here was a woman that had known many years of happiness, a woman that heaped love on every one that she knew. While she was not a tall woman by any means, her lack of height did not matter. One could easily tell that she made up for it in spirit. She smiled happily as she ran towards them. "At last the oldest of my brood is home. Now, if I can just get the wee runt home I'll be happy as can be." The accent was not exactly quite like Alec's. It was as if she had not lived in Scotland all of her life.

Alec grinned back. His face just lit up. It reminded her of Christmas morning when she was a child. A wondrous time for any child, it was far more important to her. Magic. Christmas magic. That's what Alec reminded her of. The most powerful thing in the world is magic. When had she forgotten that? Amy felt her knees go weak, so many things she had missed out on in the last few years. Why had she not realized it sooner?

Alec seemed to notice her weakness and moved his hand from behind her back to around her waist. "Lass, are ye alright?" She nodded, and he gave her a skeptical look. He kept his arm around her waist and this caused his mother to grin. Sheena, if Amy remembered correctly. Unfortunately, some of the details he had imparted upon her waking up in the hospital were still a little fuzzy. "Mum, ye know the youngest of us will be here soon and then the Inn will be too full for any guests." She shrugged before turning towards Amy. "Amy Killigan, meet my mum, Sheena MacDaniel."

Amy stuck out a hand, but Sheena pushed it aside. Sheena hugged her for all she was worth while being mindful of injuries, as if Alec had described exactly where her injuries were, so that they could be avoided. "There's no need for pleasantries, Amy Killigan. Ye are welcome as family for as long as ye want." A picture of Amy's mother flashed through her mind. Her throat clogged in response to the tears which threatened to fall. She nodded to Sheena, but Sheena seemed to understand despite no spoken words.

Sheena's hair swished as she turned to Rory, "Rory, take Amy up to the room I fixed. Let her put her stuff away. Show her the washbasin too, in case she needs it. Lass, we'll see to everything. We have a lovely spot for yer pup too. Riley could always use a friend, especially a Hellhound. Och, the trouble they will cause. Alec will see to him."

As Rory nodded and led Amy away, Sheena looked

down to Rocky. "Well, aren't ye a surprise, hound?" Rocky jumped up, knocking her back. Sheena laughed as she struggled to keep her balance under the heavy boxer. Grabbing his muzzle gently in her hands, she caressed his head. "Alec, you did right to bring that lass here. She's been hurt somethin' awful and it's not just what ye see now. Someone has done her a world of hurt that may never be able to be set right. Tis a proud day to have ye as my son."

Alec nodded, "I know, but if I can protect the lass from any more hurt that bastard might cause then tis worth it." He gazed at the door as if expecting to see Amy walk back out.

"Alec Kirk MacDaniel, no son of mine will be speakin' such filth in front of a woman." Alec lowered his head as he realized what he said. "Unfortunately, in this case the man that did that to yer lass is a bastard indeed."

"Mum, I dinnae know if he will follow."

"If the bloody bastard does then ye and yer brothers have my permission to do as ye were taught. To the full extent. Do ye understand?"

Alec wrapped his arms around his mother. "Might be needed."

"After all, what good is having a son in the Yard and a son that tis a Constable if ye boys dinnae get to use the things taught to ye?"

Alec smiled a sad smile, his mother knew his heart. However, she did not know what made it ache. He had never told her how Morvena was killed or that the babe wasn't his. His mother had never questioned him…

CHAPTER 15

AMY STEPPED INTO THE BEDROOM and forgot to breathe. There were black and white photos of a lighthouse and the ocean on one side of the room and colored pictures of sunsets above the bed. On the white iron rod bed was a white comforter with purple lilacs. There was an old oak desk in the corner of the room with a painting of a water fall. Amy walked to the window and looked out. She had a terrific view of the lighthouse that was in the pictures and it made her gasp. The lighthouse was far away, yet it was still visible. A fog was rolling in around it, giving it a strikingly eerie appearance. "It's gorgeous isn't it?"

Amy looked up at Rory. "Yes, it is." He smiled and set her two bags down. "Rory, not that I'm not grateful or anything, but why are you guys being so nice to me?"

Rory smirked. "Ye seem like a nice lass, but truth be told…Ye got Alec to look twice." She gave him a confused look and he continued, "Alec has had a rough time of it… That lad has only eyed a bonnie lass once. Don't get me wrong, he's taken a few to bed, but he's never eyed one twice."

Her eyes went wide. "No! We haven't…I mean I'm

not…It's not like…" She threw her hands up, as if to stop the thoughts that might be forming in his mind — the scenarios that might be playing out. Her face flamed with embarrassment.

"Lass, calm down, if Alec thinks yer worth it then ye are. Besides, I would give a hefty price just to see that hound of yers sit on him again." He turned and left with her staring after him.

No one had ever told her she was worth anything. She sat down on the bed and wondered if maybe she really was worth it. She wondered if maybe she deserved some happiness. "If ye keep thinking that hard somethin' might break."

She had been lost in thought for a while and the voice caused her to jump. She looked up and saw Alec standing in the doorway. "Alec, why did you bring me here?" He gave her a weird look for a second and she grew nervous. "It's not that I'm ungrateful or anything…I just can't help but wonder why you would take a total stranger home to meet your parents, much less meet your parents on a different continent."

Watching his motions, she couldn't help but stare as he crossed the few feet separating them and stood before her. The lines in his face, the creases that came with age and worry, were strained. What he would say to her next would be the truth. No matter what the words were, she would be able to believe them.

He kneeled down in between her legs and reached for her face. He cupped her chin. "Because no woman deserves what ye went through… and ye make me feel something — something different." Then he kissed her. She went completely frigid for a second until his tongue caressed her lips. She opened them against her will and felt him smile as he delved into a war with her tongue.

She closed her eyes and melted into the kiss as Alec lightly seized a handful of her hair. He used her hair to carefully pull her head back and placed light kisses along her chin as he traveled down her neck. She should stop him, but she couldn't form the words. The kisses were soft, like a butterfly's wings. Her stomach flipped in a way that it had not done in almost fifteen years. Her mind seemed to fade away as she lost herself in the onslaught of unfamiliar emotion.

Amy moaned as he began to undo the buttons on her midnight blue button up shirt. The doctor had recommended them because of her ribs. She wondered if this was the right thing to do. What would he think of her? As he undid the last button, he began to trail down the center of her chest and he stopped. She realized that he had noticed the scar along her collarbone. Fear seized her and she tried to turn away. His hand on her back stopped her. Shyly she looked up at him. His face was full of emotion, but she couldn't understand what the emotion was. Was it anger? Was it worry? It seemed a mix of both.

"Dinnae turn away from me," he whispered to her. His voice soft and pleading.

He brought his left hand up to caress her left breast as he began to lick and kiss her scar. She shuttered in response and felt his lips turn upward into a devious grin.

Amy couldn't think straight as Alec playfully bit her collarbone. She moaned and vaguely realized that she was now lying on her back with Alec in between her legs. She bit her lip and he pushed the strap of her bra down her shoulder. He brought the cloth down, exposing her left nipple. He leaned forward. Cautiously she watched him, wondering what he planned to do. Butterflies assaulted her and adrenaline kicked in as he hovered over her breast. His tongue darted out and he licked her nipple before swirling his tongue around the bud. Her head fell back and a moan escaped from between her lips. She pushed her pelvis forward in an effort to cause friction and he sucked softly, gently on the nipple.

He was moving over to the other one to give it the same attention when Amy heard a cough behind him. Alec jerked up and quickly pulled her shirt over to cover her. "Whoever is eavesdropping better make their selves known."

Oh God! How had she let it go so far? Why hadn't she stopped it? Mortified she tried to cover her face. What they must think of her... Even Alec would probably think she was a whore, just waiting to fall in bed with him. Or was that why he brought her there? All of her insecurities rose in the back of her mind.

"Uh...Alec, I wasn't sure it was safe to interrupt or not. Mum wants you and Amy downstairs for dinner." Amy could feel that her eyes were wide and her face was flushed with excitement and red from embarrassment. If only the heat coming off of her cheeks could incinerate her, then she wouldn't have to witness the fall out. "Of course I could tell her that her oldest is tryin' for a bairn." Alec groaned and Amy hid her face in his shirt. *Could this get any worse?* "You got less than five minutes to make yerselves presentable or I spill the beans."

"Tavish, I might just decide I do not need a third brother..." He left the threat hanging as he climbed off of Amy and her bed. She refused to meet his gaze as she tried to hold her shirt together. Alec sighed deeply and she watched him scrub . "Lass, I'm verra sorry." She reached out a hand for him to help her sit up. He whispered curses before shaking his head. "Amy, I forgot about yer ribs."

Amy had no idea what to say, no idea how to respond. The closest she had come to sexual encounters over the last ten years was her husband trying to force himself on her. He tried to justify it by using a bible verse, as if he had every right to do what he wanted to her.

She was unable to look at Alec, partly because she was mortified that she had let it go so far, and partly because she was afraid she had been doing something wrong — that he might not have liked what she was or wasn't doing. She also felt a deep tingle of fear that she might have enjoyed what he was doing to her just a little too much. So much time had passed since she felt drawn to someone, since she felt ready to take the next step. How had she let it go so far so fast?

Alec helped her to sit up and sighed, "I'll leave ye to freshen up. When yer ready just come down the stairs to the dinin' room."

When he left the room Amy shook her head, "kid, what did you get yourself into now?"

A few minutes later Amy made her way down the stairs and listened to the light banter going on. "Tavish, how dare ye upset her!"

"I swear I didn't know ye were makin' a move Alec!"

"Sons of mine," a voice that she didn't recognize interrupted them, "if ye don't quit that bickerin' right now I'm going to make an example out of both of ye." Amy almost laughed at that, the man reminded her so much of her father when he used to try to separate her and Finn. "Now, Alec, go check on yer lass and make sure that this wanker didn't upset the puir wee thing."

CHAPTER 16

WHEN ALEC STEPPED AROUND THE corner to go up the stairs he saw Amy a few steps up. The smile on her face caused his heart to stop and his lungs refused to obey their need for air. Her curly hair was cascading around her shoulders and the light was playing with it beautifully. Tinges of red appeared amongst the golden brown strands. Copper seemed to stand out amongst the black strands interspersed as well. So many different colors were in that mane. His fingers ached, begging to reach out and touch them. They called to him like a Siren to a sailor. Just one touch. That's all it would take to completely undo him. Alec swallowed audibly as she whispered, "So what's for dinner?"

Amy was aware that her voice sounded like she was coming on to Alec, but she couldn't help it with the look he was giving her. It was the look of a man dying of thirst in the desert who had just happened upon an oasis. He opened and closed his mouth a few times like he was trying to say something, but just couldn't make it come out. She walked down the last few steps and reached out her hand to him. "Don't worry so much, Alec, there's days I surprise myself."

Alec smiled and led her into the dining area. He seated her at the huge wooden table and sat next to her. He had her seated on the end of the table, so she wouldn't feel cramped. Her eyes went wide in amazement as she looked around at all the food. He leaned over and whispered in her ear, "It's not just us MacDaniels that eat here. The residents of the Inn and the village eat here as well. Alison's cookin' is terrific. The lass studied with French chefs for 'round four years before returnin' home to Ullapool."

Amy nodded, concentrating on trying to keep her reaction to his warm breath on her neck from showing. "So, lass, what do you do for a livin' over in America?" The voice that saved her belonged to a big man with blond hair and sea green eyes.

She stared at his figure for a minute in shock. He seemed strong enough to break the table in two, yet he held the small glass carefully. "Um…it's not much. It makes me happy though. I work at an outdoor facility. Well, I work inside, but we rent out all kinds of outdoor equipment like tents, sleeping bags, canoes, and kayaks. We also take people out into the middle of nowhere and teach them how to find their way back."

"Like orienteering?" Surprise must have shown on her face because he laughed, "Aye, tis verra important to learn the way back. So easy to get lost these days."

"Yes, it is." It was easy to get lost in more ways than one. "I've actually been working there for a little over a year."

His eyes seemed to be assessing her as he then asked, "for a year ye say? What did ye do before that?"

Amy froze like a deer in headlights and Alec seemed to

pick up on her fear. "Da', leave the puir lass alone. She's had a rough couple of days as is."

Alan frowned at his son before smiling softly at Amy. "Lass, we're a nosy sort, but if there's ever anythin' ye do not wish to speak of no one will force ye. Understood?"

She nodded. "It's not that I don't want to talk about it, it's just that when I do people have mixed emotions…"

"Well, lass, my oldest is a … was a soldier… My second is a Investigator on leave, my third is a fisherman that never brings home a catch when he is not a Constable, my fourth is a painter that never sells his paintings, an' my youngest is a college man who never studies. I am happy and proud of all of them. Nothin' could make me feel otherwise."

Amy could feel the pride in his voice for his children and the love as well. The constant ache in her chest grew. Her own parents had alway been proud of her too. It didn't matter what she had done, there was always that same pride in their voices. Sadness struck her at the loss of his first son. It was not a given that one would come back from war. Maybe he could understand… "I was in the military…"

Alec sat straighter wondering what his lass was doing there, but his father asked the question before he got the chance to. "Lass, what were ye doing fightin' wars?" His eyes clouded. They reminded her of an encroaching storm.

She frowned, "I was making my way in the world."

Rory grinned. "Och, a wee fighter ye are. Were ye Army, Marines, or Navy?"

"I'm surprised that you know the branches."

"Why?"

"Just not something I considered that would be known here." Shrugging, she decided to answer his question. "I was Navy."

"What 'twas it like?"

"The Navy? It was interesting." It was always hard to talk about her military time. Joining because she loved her country and wanted to do something great, she had never expected her military journey to go so astray. "What would you like to know?"

"What did ye do in the Navy?'

"I spent a year on an aircraft carrier in Mayport, Florida before I was transferred to shore for six months training in Pensacola, Florida. After I completed it I spent another year on another aircraft carrier, out of San Diego, California. Then I was transferred to a small research vessel out of Bahrain..." She subconsciously reached up to where her scar was slightly visible from her shirt and let her hand rest there. Lost in memories.

Alec frowned, but said nothing. Tavish, who seemed to be in awe that the small lass his brother had taken such a liking to was a sailor, decided to make a joke. "So did ye meet any pirates other than our Alec?" She looked up sharply; her face was filled with fright. In that second Alec would have given anything to force Tavish to take that question back, to wipe the slate clean by reversing time. Amy jumped up from her chair when Alec lightly touched her elbow. She knocked the chair over in her haste to get away and tears began streaming down her cheeks as she ran from the room.

Alec turned a look of pure malice on Tavish, but before he could jump across the table to maim him Sheena intervened. Sheena smacked Tavish upside his head and looked at Alec. "Go after yer lass before she gets into trouble on account of this wanker."

Alec didn't need to be told twice. As he went after her he wondered what made her so frightened in that single moment. As he ascended the stairs he thought about what he was going to say. Once he reached her door, which was now shut and locked, he knocked quietly. "Amy," he called. "Lass, my brother is verra sorry for what he said. He dinna mean anything by it. Please let me in? Please say yer alright?" He stood there listening to the silence coming from the room for a while. "Lass, no matter what we say to ye, ye are safe here. I have vowed it and my brothers, as idiotic as they may be, will help keep my vow to ye. Tis no harm meant by any words said tonight."

As Alec returned downstairs his father pulled him into the kitchen to finish their meal. "Alec, my boy, it's high time I let ye in on a secret…Us, MacDaniels, there is somethin' special. Somethin' that we have passed from da' to son for generations now. A secret fer when we find that special lass. The one meant fer us. I remember when yer grandda' saw me eyein' yer mum." Alan's face took on an elf-like quality as he remembered a wonderful moment in time.

"Why not mention this when I married Morvena?"

"Son, I love ye with every breath in my body, however, she twas not meant for ye." With a deep sigh he began, "I'll tell ye the same ye grandda' told to me. 'When ye find the lass of yer dreams, come what may, hold on to her with a strength that surpasses any man's will to take her. If she runs, run faster, if she cries, soothe harder, if she laughs, make it happen again, and above all if her eye shall stray carry her off to bed before she can take a step towards where she's lookin'.' That right there is what I have lived by fer the last thirty years and kept yer mum by my side."

Alec smiled as he remembered a time when he was six and his mother had smiled at Doctor McCoy. His father had seen it and snarled right before he threw his mother over his shoulder to carry home. He saw neither hide nor hair of them for thirteen hours afterwards. His grandda' had just laughed and said "Tis the MacDaniel way my boy...Tis the MacDaniel way." Nine months later Ian was born.

His father's voice brought him back from the memories. "I'm tellin' ye, Alec, that lass is a fiery one that I would be right proud to call daughter. Keep the Mac-Daniel way in mind and ye'll have a happy marriage."

"Da' be that as it may, she is already married."

"The day he first hurt her she was no longer his, in my book. That lass is free for the takin'. An whether there be a weddin' or not she is welcome, as family, and we will be proud to call her such."

CHAPTER 17

AMY STOOD AT THE OPEN window, with one foot out of it, looking at the door. She sighed in regret. For a moment she had felt as if she truly belonged. The never ending fear had seemed to finally ease, even disappear. They were such wonderful people. Despite the fact that they had lost so much, they were truly good. Why taint them with the horrors she had seen? The horrors she would bring?

She could feel a deep within her chest. Her father had been a good man and her mother had been a good woman. They had been so proud of her when she announced that she was joining the Navy, proud that she had done what she felt was right, despite the danger. Well, it was time to do what was right again. It was a mistake to come to Scotland. It was a mistake to trust Alec. He had a family. Hers was long gone. Rocky was all that she had left, but Matthew would not harm him. Alec's family was free for the marking though. He would go after them with everything he had. She could never let them be harmed because of her. She still ached at the loss of Finn. Why were so many people being harmed over her? When she had not done what Matthew suspected she had… after the agent's death she hadn't told a soul about the trade routes. How could she?

She whispered, "Alec, you have no idea what you're getting into." It was true. He was a good man, but he had no idea. Maybe in a different life they could have been more. If only she had met him first. There was no time for what-ifs or could have beens though. There was only the was, the is, and the will be. None of that included Alec. None of that included his wonderful family — the wonderful family that reminded her of Christmas mornings as a child, loving memories with her own family — memories that were long gone, and it was all her fault.

"You have no idea who I am or what I've done… I'm trouble and regret. Nothing more." She shook her head and looked back down at the ground. She swung her other foot over the window sill and swallowed. "Remember, Ames, it's just like jumping off the diving board at boot camp… Except now you're landing on the hard unforgiving ground instead of the stinging water…" Taking in an exaggeratedly deep breath in an attempt to calm the butterflies in her stomach did nothing but delay the inevitable. Either she was going to jump or she was going stay. Either way there was pain involved. It was better to chose the least painful route. Slowly releasing the breath she held gave her a smidgeon of courage. The least painful one it is. "Well, here goes nothing," she said as she dropped the two stories to the ground.

She landed with her knees bent, immediately going into a roll just as she had been taught many years ago. As she stood up with a hand on her side and pain in her eyes she looked up at the house. It would be hours before they learned of her disappearance. That would buy her some time. At least, she hoped it would. The light in Alec's eyes when he had kissed her was something to be reckoned with. He was just trying to help her, wasn't he? Or did he want something else?

"Alec MacDaniel, you're safer without me around. I just hope you take care of Rocky for me." A flash of lightning tore across the sky as she turned and began walking away from the house. "Should have stayed in the states. At least there I know the terrain." It's not like this was the first time she was in unfamiliar territory. This was not even the first time that the threats were unknown.

Reaching up she pressed down on her collar bone. It still ached when she thought about it. So many years later and she could still feel the sting of the salt water on her wounds. Matthew knew what she had done. The DEA made a deal and got her transferred to the research vessel out of Bahrain. It was just temporary until the bust was done, that way she couldn't be blamed for what happened. Matthew had blamed her though. His drug runner boss had too. Tracked her down all the way in the Gulf… The vessel was attacked. Pirates. They were everywhere.

The Pirates that had been hired had thought her dead when they tossed her overboard. They had finished with her, and she was no good to them. Three days in the ocean. Three days floating on her back, trying to make it to shore or to another Navy vessel. It was a wonder that the sharks or sea snakes had not gotten to her before the tanker found her. They had claimed that luck was on her side. Well, if luck really existed, and had her back, then she would find her way back all by herself. Steeling herself she raised her chin defiantly. Yep, she would find her way back and figure out some way to beat Matthew without Alec's help. It was insane of her to even have agreed to come to Scotland…

CHAPTER 18

THREE HOURS LATER AMY WAS questioning just what she had done to deserve this. Shivering from hours of being cold and wet had brought about a self-anger unlike anything human. Her clothes were soaked and sticking to her skin. She could see her own breath and was pretty sure that the temperature had dropped dramatically since their arrival. Her anger level had reached Angry Little Troll level. That was the equivalent of DefCon Five.

Kicking at a poor defenseless rock on the road she screamed, "Stupid! Just couldn't grab a jacket could we!?! Oh, no! Just had to be all big and bad when they start asking scary questions! Cause that's how we roll! God, I am a moron…" She cast a quick glance up to the sky as if waiting for God to confirm it. A streak of lightning was her answer. Definitely a moron.

Wrapping her arms tighter around her, hoping that it would magically quell the cold, she continued walking down the road that nobody apparently seemed to ever drive down. Where in the world were all the cars? Or was she the only one out in this weather. Giving a sarcastic snort, she corrected herself. The only idiot out in this weather…

A little voice in her head seemed to be laughing at her. She had never been to Scotland before, and upon learning that she was coming to a foreign country that she's been dying to visit for years she did not even bother to try to research anything about the climate, people, or routes. She knew she was in the Highlands, but that essentially told her nothing. Well, nothing modernly significant. She knew the history of the land and the people. Bunch of good that did her now. "Next time let's look up modern history before we go on a jaunt, hn, Ames", she reprimanded herself.

Coming to a halt she threw up her arms towards the sky, "How big of a moron am I to let some strange guy bring me almost half way across the world!?!" Shouting it didn't seem to help. It did make her feel a bit better though. When in doubt, shout. The motto still made her giggle. She could not remember where she had first heard it, but it had stuck with her for all these years.

"Seriously?" She threw her arms up in frustration. "Where the hell am I?" Then she heard it, a car. The sound was soft, but was getting louder. It was coming her way!

She heard the little blue mini coop seconds before she saw it and almost wept. Finally someone was driving along the little road. She began waving to get the driver to stop. As the car grew closer it showed no signs of slowing down. She squinted her eyes to see better and noticed that the driver was looking in the glove box, not at the road, not in the direction that he was going. Her eyes went wide in fear; she was standing in the middle of the road trying to get his attention. Dear God! He was going to hit her!

The driver looked up just in time to see her turn and hunch her shoulders, waiting for him to hit her. He grabbed the wheel with both hands and jerked it to the right. He narrowly missed her as he slammed on the breaks and veered slightly off the road. The second he came to a stop he jumped out, "Are ye alright," he screamed! She looked at him in shock. What was she doing in the road? Her mouth opened and closed several times before her eyes rolled back into her head and she collapsed into a heap. Oh dear Lord! He killed her!

Instincts kicked in and he ran over towards her. As he got close he began crouching while still running and slid next to her. Quickly turning her towards him he prayed that she was still alive, holding his breath as he began feeling for a pulse. A light thready thump greeted him. He sighed in relief upon finding one.

He took deep breaths to calm himself before he took in her appearance. She was sopping wet from head to toe, her black Keds were covered in mud, her cotton black pants were covered up to the knee in mud, and her midnight blue button up shirt was missing a button and had specks of mud on it. Her hands were also covered in mud and had left some muddy hand prints on her blouse.

"Wee thing, what in the world are ye doin' out here?" He knew for a fact that the road he was traveling on was a back road from Inverness and since it took an extra half hour it was not traveled as much. The Inn was the closest place around actually. Maybe she was a tourist staying there and had gotten lost. That would explain her state, but where was her jacket?

He reached down and casually picked her up. She was so light. "I'll take ye to Mum, she'll know what to do." Mum always knew what to do. It did not matter whether it was a broken heart or a broken arm, she always knew what to do. The disappearance of Danny had hit her hard though, even if she refused to let it show. If they ever found him she would kill him. That much was for sure.

Although, at the moment Ian figured she was more inclined to kill him first... Maybe he should have skipped the prank. It was probably a bad idea at any time, but it was probably a disastrous idea to even have contemplated with everything going on. Maybe he could plead temporary insanity now that he thought about it, especially at such a trying time. Poor Alec. So much had changed for him in such a short time. Maybe Mum would forgive him in light of everything, or she would be distracted by the woman that needed their help.

As he settled the woman in the passenger's side of the car he nodded. Yes, she would be distracted. That would save his hide for a bit, or earn him a more unpleasant death once he told how he almost ran her own. Scrunching up his face in anticipation of the gruesomeness he decided to leave that part out. He was already in trouble. Why make it worse?

CHAPTER 19

THE FIRST COHERENT THOUGHT AMY could muster was that she felt warm and dry. Reaching for it she felt the blanket. It was a warm soft cotton. Fisting the blanket, she brought it closer to her chin to further curl into it. She sighed, content. "Lass," the Scottish brogue shocked her fully awake. "If ye ever pull a stunt like that 'gain I will have ye tied down to a bed for the rest of yer days." The voice was dangerous and caused a thrill of excitement to rush through her. Opening her eyes she found Alec MacDaniel leaning against the wall, his ice blue eyes were focused and dangerously narrowed on her. She gulped and he pushed himself off the wall. He stalked towards her. "What do ye think ye were doing?"

Trying to bury herself underneath the blanket, hoping it would provide protection against his anger she was surprised when he reached out and jerked it completely off of her. "I asked ye a question and I expect an answer." She gulped again and found it hard to breathe. He looked so dangerous and she began to feel terror. It snaked through her gut and coiled around her heart. However, a funny little thought popped into her mind. He was like an angry teddy bear. The image caused her to grin.

"Ye could 'ave died, Amy. Do ye not understand that?"

She did, but it was too much. She reached up a hand and his features softened. A realization struck her hard. She was not afraid of him, not exactly, but rather what he could make her feel. What he was going to make her body feel. He leaned over her and she rolled onto her back. Then she attempted to melt into the mattress. "Answer me," he demanded softly. "What were ye doing?"

She opened her mouth, but no sound would come out. Then he did something that shocked her and thrilled her at the same time. He climbed onto the bed and straddled her hips. She looked down to where he was sitting on her and realized that her clothes were missing. She was only wearing a bra and panties. A fire lit in her lower belly and she croaked out, "Running away."

Alec knew that he had her in between a rock and a hard place. There was no way he could not possibly know that. It seemed that he was willing to do what was necessary to show her that he meant business and he had her right where he wanted her. Her lungs refused to accept air as he reached a strong hand downward and gently dragged a finger in between her breasts. He looked pleased when he saw the desire radiating from her hazel eyes. "Yer eyes, such beauty. The gold flakes call to me. Such abundance." He leaned down and sensually licked her neck, "why would ye be runnin' away when this is so much more fun?"

'Why indeed,' Amy thought. She tried to move, but was stopped when he unclasped her black silk bra. It was her only front opening bra. She had been so sore that it had just made things easier to wear it. Maybe she was subconsciously planning ahead. He pushed it open and stared at her. He licked his lips and her brain went hay-wire. "Um…Uh…"

Alec smiled at her loss for words. He then cupped her right breast, "I believe this is where we left off last time, no?" He watched her eyes drift close as she bit her lip. "How does this feel, love?"

She opened her mouth to say something, but it was lost in a ragged moan as he closed his mouth over her nipple. Floored by the sound Alec cupped the other one and rubbed the tip with his thumb. Her eyes flew open, filled with lust. Alec leaned back and rearranged himself so that he was in between her legs he whispered, "Cross yer ankles 'round my waist."

Amy had no control over herself as she did his biding. She brushed her heat against his arousal and gasped, then as if possessed began pushing at his jeans. He chuckled as she unbuttoned them and undid the fly with nimble fingers. She blushed at his laughter thinking it was directed at her in an ill light. It had been so long. Maybe she had done something wrong. She uncrossed her ankles and snatched her fingers back to herself while redirecting her eyes in shame.

Alec frowned. "Lass, dinna think to run from me, I meant nothin' by it. Ye should feel no shame in this and if ye wish to stop we will." After a second her eyes returned to his, seeking truth to his words. There was nothing in them or on his face to illustrate that she should be embarrassed. She nodded. Trust, trust was important. It had to be earned though and this was the perfect chance for him to earn it. He grinned. "I promise if nothin' else, ye will enjoy this." She gave him a skeptical look, but said not a word as she tugged on his shirt. With a grin, he sat up part way, and pulled it over his head. Her eyes widened slightly at his chiseled physique.

His abs had abs.

"The pants too?" She whispered, still unsure of herself. The lust was plain as she licked her lips. He stood up off the bed and quickly pushed them down to his ankles, never taking his eyes off of hers. She stared at his erect manhood with wide eyes. Maybe this was a bad idea. Logically she knew everything would work out well, but the remembered pain resurfaced. The pain would forever be ingrained in her memory… Quickly quelling it, she focused on the lust. The lust would help.

"Do ye like what ye see, Amy?"

Amy shuddered when he said her name. It came out as "Aimee" and she had never heard her name sound so sexy before. She raised a hand and beckoned him closer with a thin finger. "Please, say it again?"

He raised an eyebrow, "Which part?" He smiled to show he was teasing as he stepped out of the jeans and climbed back on the bed.

"My name. Please say my name again."

He climbed in between her legs, leaned down and whispered, "Amy, do you want this?" He grabbed her by her shoulders and pulled down so that she was roughly pulled against his arousal. She moaned in delight as the fire began to burn brighter, the contact sending a pulse deep within her and the heat raged. Alec grinned wickedly as he began a trail of kisses from her neck down her chest to her black silk panties. He murmured, "Tis such a waste."

"Wha…What is?"

He leaned back and pushed a finger into the side of her underwear. She was certain that he could feel the heat and wetness emanating from her core as he lightly caressed her. At the touch she bucked and whined for more. He whispered, "This…," and ripped her panties from her body. At that simple act she rode straight over the mountain and began a descent into orgasm. Her toes curled. Her body shook with its ferocity and Alec seemed to grow tighter with need and want.

Alec quickly shed his boxer shorts and feasted his eyes upon her. Amy's eyes were closed in bliss as she finished riding the wave. He leaned down and began to kiss her hip bones, "There's more," she questioned?

"Of course, Amy, after all there are at least eight hours of night on this night that we may work with. There is much to show ye. Much to learn. Tis simply the beginning." He whispered, "And eight hours of night every other night for the rest of our lives." She looked at him then with a mixed expression of confusion and hope. She had to have heard him wrong.

The trail of kisses moved closer to her heat and she tensed. He placed his hands on her knees to stop her reaction of closing her legs together. "Please, dinnae fear me." At that simple demand she gave in. She relaxed her body and just felt. She felt Alec's whiskers scratch her skin in an erotic way as he began to kiss her where no man had ever dared to. Pressure mounted as his tongue swirled around her clit. She fisted the bed sheets and slammed her mouth shut. He wrapped his arms around her upper thighs and pulled her closer. He felt her grow hotter and wetter as he slid his tongue into her opening. A scream tore from her as the pressure mounted to an almost intolerable throb. "Please...," she begged.

The knowledge that she was ready for him was plain as the air he was breathing, but Alec wasn't through with her yet. "Amy, I can get one more from ye..." She whimpered as he nipped her inner thigh then he went right back to caressing her with his tongue. As he did that he lightly traced her right nipple with one hand and used the other to insert a finger in her. She whimpered once again nearly crazy with need as he used it on her. Her whole body was on fire and tensed ready for attack then did the one thing he never expected in a million years.

She growled, reached down and grabbed his upper arms. She pulled him up to her, rolled them over, and sank herself deep onto him in one fluid motion. It felt wonderful. He fit so perfectly. She sighed in relief as she began a rhythm of movements. Alec was shocked at her tightness and the heat. It felt so perfect for him to be there. As he recovered from the shock of her actions he grabbed her waist. She shivered as he looked up at her. Knowing that he was watching in rapt fascination was such a powerful aphrodisiac. As she threw her head back and rode him for all she was worth she thought that this was it, this was what sex was supposed to be about. It was supposed to be about feeling beautiful. She looked as beautiful as a Siren with her curly hair bouncing in the moonlight. He felt her muscles clench as she bit her lip. She came with a smile and a tiny moan. However, she didn't stop. She kept moving and Alec felt himself about to come. He gripped her waist tighter as he tried to hold back.

Amy's body was still wound tight as she continued to writhe and move on Alec's hardness. She could sense he was going to come soon from his movements and wanted to make sure it was as good for him as it was for her. Her body had a light sheen of sweat from the work, but she had never felt so good. With one last roll of her hips Alec's strength deserted him and he came violently into her. Even in his orgasmic bliss he noticed that she was shuddering from climaxing as well and couldn't keep the smug grin from his face. He found it oddly endearing that as they were climaxing in sequence she had whispered his name. It was a throaty whisper that left him dying to hear it again. He rolled them to the side and she gave him a sleepy seductive smile. "Close yer eyes, Amy, I'll be here when ye wake."

She wrapped an arm tight around his waist and whispered, "You promise?" He kissed the top of her head and replied that he would. He stayed sheathed within her as she drifted off to sleep and he held her close as he thought. Alec had just found his other half, yet he couldn't have her in marriage because she was already someone else's. That thought tore his heart in two as his eyes drifted shut without his consent and he joined her in sleep.

CHAPTER 20

UPON WAKING, IT BECAME OBVIOUS that it had been a long time since Amy had been with anyone. The nightmares she suffered… They were enough to bring any man to his knees from helplessness. Her muscles stayed taunt most of the night. Her feet kicked as if she was trying to run away. Tears even ran down her cheeks. Each time he had held her, soothed her, and kissed away her tears. It was not enough though.

What exactly had she been through? He had imagined that it had been awful, but it seemed as if he had barely scratched the surface. Had she never been appreciated as a woman? Had she never been shown just how beautiful she is? Had she never been teased wantonly and brought to climax while shouting her lover's name? Or shown the finer side of ecstasy? Had a man ever shown her that she was worth spending time with? For no other reason than to be by her side? Did she know what she was missing? Had she guessed?

Hours of tossing and turning had made him desire to show her all of these things. The trouble how to show her without her realizing just how much she had lost over the years. Fortunately, she had finally settled down while wrapped in his arms, only after a light kiss to her forehead though.

A light sigh drew him back to focus on her. Now that the lines in her face had smoothed out, peace reflected back at him. Her curls were now the size of French tendrils. Perfectly cylindrical, it would wrap tightly around his fingers if he dared.

Maybe it was time that she had a bit of fun. Where would he want to go if it was his first time visiting Scotland? Where would he have fun? Maybe he could take her sightseeing? Grinning at the thought, he decided that she could definitely use some sightseeing. Only, where? Not knowing much about the pixie made it hard to decide what to go see. Maybe she'd like to shop. Morvena loved to shop. So far she had proven to be so different from Morvena though. So very different.

There that little sigh was again. The little sounds she made in her sleep brought a grin to his face. She seemed so simple, like the world was simple. Right and wrong was fairly defined. The gray line did not bend with her. So very different than Morvena indeed.

Those beautiful hazel eyes opened up. Amy deserved so much more than what he could give. If he could give her a bit of happiness then he would. The bastard could already be on his way for her. Might as well start soon. "Beautiful lass. What would ye like to see today?"

"Hn?"

"Ye mentioned that ye had never before seen Scotland. What would ye like to see?"

"I don't understand…"

"Would ye like to go shoppin'? In town?"

Her face scrunched up, as he suspected it would. "I don't know much about shopping. I don't understand what's going on…"

"What do ye not understand?"

"Why would you want to take me anywhere?"

Why would he...? His heart stopped as realization dawned. Had no one ever taken her anywhere just to spend time with her? He knew that she had been on her own for a while, but... Did no one spend time with her?

Maybe not. She had not mentioned any other family. Her only brother had been killed by the man hunting her. Did she not have any friends? Perhaps she did not feel that it was safe to have friends. Who would if they were in her place... What would it be like to be so alone? Steeling himself against the sadness he felt he cleared his throat. "Ye mentioned that ye worked outdoors. A hike might be a fine idea?"

"A hike?"

"Aye, a hike. What do ye think, Amy?"

Her grin was all the answer he needed. Measach would be the perfect place. The Falls would be beautiful and quiet this time of year.

Maybe it was time to lay some ghosts to rest. Hers and his.

CHAPTER 21

LOOKING OUT OVER THE FALLS, it seemed as if everything was perfect, as if there were no troubles in the world that could harm them, as if none existed, but deep down she knew trouble would find them soon. Alec was delusional if he truly believed that Matthew would stop just because she fled the country, not with what she knew.

A slight mist rose up from below. The light hit it just right, creating the appearance of a rainbow. The weather was slightly cool, but she barely felt the chill. Tilting her head down to take in her appearance, she sighed. They should have packed hiking boots for her, just in case. The tennis shoes on her feet had long since been at the end of their life, it was just hard to get rid of them. Unbelievably, they had once been white. Now they were dishwater grey with a hint of southern red clay. At least the jeans and hooded sweatshirt had been a good thing for them to pack for her.

Hearing Alec behind her she turned, gracing him with a smile. "This is such a beautiful place."

"Tis been many years since I 'ave been here. A tourist place now."

"Sometimes tourist places lose the magic that made them popular. Other times it enhances it. Why is there no one here today?"

"Tis not yet the season for tourists. Most are running amuck in the large cities this time of year."

"Can we go anywhere?" He nodded and she felt slightly giddy. "Can we go down there?" Pointing below to the base of the falls she gave a little sigh. It was a dream of hers to feel the water cascading down. The strength in the water had always amazed her. Even as a small child she had dreamed to one day place her hand within the stream of the falls. Niagra Falls had always been out of reach in the states. The Falls of Mesach were smaller though, more confined, perfect for someone wanting to reach out and touch the water.

"Aye, anywhere ye like. The moss tis slippery though."

"How do we get down?"

His grin seemed roguish, teasing perhaps, but with a hint of something else — something dangerous, not physically dangerous, but dangerous to her heart — the heart that had remained dormant and protected for so long. Out of safety more than anything else, she had encased it in ice, yet this man seemed to know the secret. He could make the ice thaw as a pond thaws in spring.

Ice when thawing was dangerous indeed. If one was not careful they would be sucked beneath and trapped, struggling for breath, waiting for the heart and brain to catch up with the lungs. Waiting to die, as there was no escape...

This man would be easy to fall in love with if she was not careful. Love was a tricky thing. There was no escaping it once it was found. Would she fly with him or would she be trapped beneath the ice? There was only one way to find out.

"Alec, please show me the way." Holding out her hand to him was such a hard thing to do. Relief flooded her when he took it. No hesitation, he just took it. Maybe everything would be alright after all.

"Aye, I would be happy to."

As they proceeded across the bridge to the other side Amy noticed what looked like a pathway down. It was slightly hidden amongst the craggy rocks, but it was there. It had been so long since she had an adventure, especially one with such a hot man. Why was she not afraid of him? Last night had been so easy going, filled with heat and passion. In fact, just thinking about it made her want to pull him aside and…

"Lass, yer looking like ye want to jump me."

Stopping suddenly she realized that he was looking at her the same way. "I… uh…"

Pulling her to him, he embraced her. "Later. For now we shall see the falls." Turning back he once again grabbed her hand. "Tis amazing at the base." The entrance to the path was hidden by bushes. It felt forbidden to cross it, but they did. "Amy, the Falls hold many secrets. Secrets between lovers. Secrets between friends. Mayhap one day we shall be both."

"I thought you said you'd take me down the path."

"Aye, indeed I did. Will ye allow me a kiss first?" She answered him with a grin. Pulling her close, he placed his right hand on the side of her head, using his thumb to caress her face. "Yer beautiful woman. Never let any man tell ye different."

Leaning forward he kissed her gently on the lips. As her eyes closed he kissed her again, slowly letting passion seep forth. Slowly, as if learning to trust anew, her lips parted. He stepped forward, pulling her against him. His hand moved to behind her head, his fingers intwined in her hair. His other hand slid around her waist and settled in the middle of her back. The sounds of the water cascading down the falls were muted as she fell into the kiss, praying it would never end. As Alec pulled back she was thankful he left his arms around her. For some reason her legs were shaky, threatening to give way. "Such a beauty ye are."

Once her legs were steady he released her. The intimate moment was broken, severed, as if it had never been. Pushing the bushes aside, Alec stepped onto the path. While his back was turned her fingers found their way to her lips. Electric. The kiss was electric. Pure and simple. Dangerous indeed. Sex on two legs, but dangerous. Her lips curved upward into a predatory smile.

"Come, Amy, the Falls await."

Following him was a simple thing. Her body shouted at her to trust him. What harm could there be in that? A lot actually, but maybe it was time to trust someone. Faith was a powerful thing. It was hard to know whether you truly had it or not unless it was tested.

The path was surprisingly steep. After a few feet the soft ground filtered out into small boulders. Climbing over them was difficult in the tennis shoes. It would have been easy in her hiking boots. Their tread was much better. Those were sitting in the mud room of her small home back in the states. No use wishing for them now.

The leaves were so pretty. Red, yellow, and golden hues all blended together to create a symphony of color. The sound of the water rushing along filtered up to her ears, reminding her of the rapids in Colorado. The wildlife there was infinitely more dangerous. Did they even have snakes here?

There were more pressing concerns on hand. The path they traversed was right on the edge. Looking down the side of the canyon made her stomach drop, such a long way down. Better not fall, because if you did then there was a chance you would never be found, or at least you would never be recognized if you were found.

———— ❦ ————

Crack! The thunder was a shock as the sky was clear. Something slammed into the ground near her. "What the…" Crack! Something slammed above her, knocking debris loose. Crouching low to the ground she heard Alec scream her name. Little rocks came sliding down the side of the path. The angle was steep. Crack! The ground began to shake as the little rocks grew in size and number. Thousands were headed her way. There was no where to go! Standing frozen in their path she watched helplessly as the distance between herself and the rocks closed. As they slammed into her feet she screamed. Flying forward she landed on the rocks, yet they continued to move. They carried her along their path. Turning her head she screamed again. She was going off the path! Over the side!

Turning back, she saw Alec's face. Terror. It was written plainly as he raced to reach her. Reaching out frantically, she grabbed at the ground, trying to hold on to anything before it was too late. There was nothing, nothing to grab on to, nothing to save her. Over the side she went, still reaching blindly, trying to grab purchase.

As she went over the side her throat shut down. The terror seemed to freeze her vocal cords. Small branches scraped at her, tearing her clothes. Grasping at anything she could, she kept falling and sliding. Finally there was a rock large enough for her to grab onto. Her fingers grated on the rough surface as she caught it and held onto the small boulder as if her life depended on it, because it did.

Gasping for breath, she couldn't focus. The ground was so far down!

"Hold on! I am coming for ye!" The rock she held on to rocked slightly. It was amazing that it held for this long. "Talk to me! Let me know yer safe!"

How could she talk to him? Her voice wouldn't work. Did he not understand? The thunder that scared her was not thunder. It sounded like a gunshot. Could it have been one? Had Matthew found her? Why had he missed her? He was such a good shot.

Oh no! Was he going to hurt Alec? What would she do if he did… She could not lose anyone else. It was too much.

"Lass! I will throttle ye if ye dinnae answer me!"

"You wouldn't dare!" The shock of his threat finally shook the hold on her vocal cords lose.

His sigh told her she was right. He would not dare harm her ever. "Are ye injured?"

"No." The rock slid as if it was giving way. "Alec, if I fall…"

"Ye willnae fall!"

"If I do!" Her heart was racing. Exhaling deeply she started over, "If I do, please look after Rocky. He needs looking after. Trouble seems to know where he is at all times."

"Ye willna fall. I am coming." The tone of his voice was set, determined. It was as if he really believed what he said. "Hold on and ye will be fine."

She could hear him moving above her, not far away. Her eyes closed in fear. He would not make it in time.

There was no way. At least he would be safe though. Matthew would leave him alone if she died. There was no need to harm Alec if she was dead.

The thunder crackled again as something slammed into the rock she held on to. Pieces of the rock splintered causing her to let go. Everything would be ok. It had to be. Alec would be safe.

A strong calloused hand wrapped around her wrist.

Her eyes shot open. Alec! He had saved her! He had put himself in danger for her.

"No! He's out there! He'll shoot you too!"

Alec ignored her and began pulling her up. "Wrap yer arms around my neck!" As soon as she got close enough she wrapped her free hand around his neck. Quickly he released her wrist, moving his hand to her waist. His hand and arm held her steady while she threw her other hand around his neck. "Good. Now hold tight. Ye hear me?" Her voice once again failed her, so she nodded. He kept his promise. Tears flooded her eyes. "Lass, ye cannae cry yet. I am not yet finished savin' ye." The smile on his lips cinched it. Her heart was stolen, stolen by a man that could do the impossible, by a man that could save her, that could make everything alright, despite the odds. She had found a man that held more worth in his soul than than there were stars in the sky.

If only she had met him years ago, before she was damaged. Maybe then her life would be different, beautiful. Maybe... Maybe she could tell him that he had just accomplished the impossible. He had saved her and in doing so kept his word. It was going to get him killed. Matthew would see to it. He would kill Alec and make her watch, just like he had killed Finn.

CHAPTER 22

ALEC STARED AT HER. SUCH a temper she had. Such a spitfire. She had almost been killed and here she was hollering at him, for saving her, of all things! What would she prefer for him to have done? Let her drop? The fall would have killed her! Was that what she wanted?

"Don't you get it!?! He's here! He crossed the freaking ocean to chase me! He's never going to stop. Never!"

He stepped backwards as she threw her arms about. She was truly mad, madder than he had ever seen a woman before. Hell, she was madder than anyone he had ever known. She would truly be a hellfire when needed. He accidentally let a grin slip at that thought.

"Alec, you don't get it, you idiot." First time anyone had ever called him an idiot. "He swore that he would kill me and he is dead set that he's going to. I don't want him to hurt you too. You could have been killed!" She covered her eyes with her hands, "I never should have left the states! What was I thinking coming here with you… I must be an idiot! You would think I'd have learned after Finn, but no. Seems I'm never going to learn."

"Are ye finished beratin' yerself?"

Her hands flew away from her face, "No, no I'm not.

I'm not berating myself either. I'm berating you! You may be some big, bad fighter, but Matthew has years of experience on his side. The Navy taught him everything he needed to know to kill someone. The only reason he didn't kill us just now is because he's toying with us. Do you understand? He's toying with me through you!"

Turning away from him she wrapped her arms around herself. The motion made him step back. How could she go from angry to sad so quickly? Unless... she had realized that she was scared, not for herself, but for him. Maybe she had finally realized that someone was going to fight for her... and it scared her. Hope surged through him. Cautiously, Alec stepped up behind her and placed his hands on her slim shoulders, in hopes that he could pass along some of his strength to her. Her countenance seemed so sad. It was as if she had lost everything with no hope of any of it ever being found. How could he tell her that he understood? That the words, though unsaid, had been heard?

"Amy, we are both safe." He turned her around in his arms, to face him. Tears graced her cheeks. So many tears she had cried and now she was crying for him. Wrapping his arms around her fully, hugging her to him, gave him the strength needed. Would it pass to her?

"Alec, I need you to understand this. He's far from done. There's more to come. That was just... That was just an appetizer, something to wet his appetite while he waits, while he creates more fear, while we wait for him to come."

Stepping forward he pulled her into a hug. "Ye give him too much power. Dinnae let him have the strength from yer weary bones."

"He's taken all the strength I have. He's taken it by force."

She sounded like she had given up. "Och, such a brave lass. Ye have more strength than ye even know." If she needed more strength then she could have all that he possessed.

"You, Alec, are a liar." Her laugh threw him for a loop. It was so unexpected, but it seemed that he had helped calm her.

"I am no more a liar than ye are a dream."

"I am no one's dream."

"Och, who is the liar now?" His eyes softened. She truly had no idea. "Come, we must get home. We must clean ye up." His brothers also needed to be made aware of the danger. The bastard had followed them. As outlandish as it was, the bastard had followed. He would protect her. When he saw her go down his heart froze. The wound in his side burned, but he would not trade it, not for anything. Barely reaching her in time, he had slid forward to catch her wrist. Probably just caught his side on a root growing up out of the ground or a stray rock. It would be hard to hide it from her. He had to try though, for her sake he had to try.

CHAPTER 23

THE NEXT MORNING AMY WOKE as the first rays of sunshine were filtering through the window. She smiled at Alec with love in her eyes. She wondered if this was how people felt when they were in love. Slightly jumping at the thought, she froze as Alec muttered in his sleep.

This man was different. Ironic that her heart knew it before her brain. Without a shadow of doubt, Alec had her heart. She had been 'married' for six years, yet her husband had never managed to win it. She lightly caressed Alec's face and her smile grew brighter when he turned into her hand. She untangled herself from him quietly and got up from the bed. She smirked when he frowned at the loss of heat. She threw on his shirt and boxers and quietly slipped out of the room, hoping he would sleep for a while longer.

Stealthily she crept down the hallway and the stairs. Seeing Sheena at the front desk she smiled before realizing her lack of clothing. Her face grew bright red and Sheena laughed. "My dear, there's nothin' to be ashamed of. The entire place heard yer lovin' last night." *Oh God, they all heard?* Sheena laughed harder as Amy lowered her eyes to the plush beige carpet. "Dear, we loved it. There's nothin' greater between a man an' a woman save lovemakin'. Tis been far too long since Alec had a lass to make him a better man."

"I'm sorry that we were so loud," Amy said meekly. She had never even considered that someone might hear them. What would they think of her?

"Lass, there were others doin' the same here last night. Yer not the only couple. Out of ye all, the only one I would box is my wee runt. The wanker knows better…" Amy nodded in understanding. Sheena walked around the desk and gave her a hug, "Dear, 'tis natural, dinna fret."

Amy nodded again and cleared her throat to change the subject. "Sheena, do you have a phone I could use to call stateside? Also do you know where I might be able to get something faxed?"

"Love, ye can use anythin' ye like." Sheena took her to the back office and showed her how it worked before leaving her alone.

Once Sheena had closed the door she picked up the phone. Her fingers itched. Nervously she dialed a number she had long since memorized. On the third ring it was answered and Amy steeled herself. "My name is Amy Lee Killigan and I need a copy of the Decree for case DV–2005–0071 faxed to…"

As Amy hung up the phone she felt a weight lifted off of her shoulders. The fax would come in any second, then she would tell Alec everything. The truth about it all. She would talk until her throat was dry and hoarse before talking some more. She was going to reveal her greatest secret. It was time. He deserved to know. It felt nerve-wracking and exciting at the same time. The secret she had kept for a little over three years was finally going to come to light, she grinned. He might not understand at first, but he would before she was done. There had been so much at risk if it had ever come to light, but now, now it was worth telling. It was worth risking an angry dragon over. A beep sounded from the fax machine as the paper came through.

The paper finished printing and she picked it up from the tray. She smiled again as she read it. Then she felt a draft as the paper slipped from her fingers and floated towards the ground. The draft hit it once again and it floated between the desk and the wall. Amy frowned, such a strange wind. As she reached down behind the desk to grab it she wondered about it. Just a bit more and she would have it. Her fingers were almost on it when her head was roughly pulled upright by a hand in her hair. Before she could gasp, a knife was pressed to her throat. The screamed died in her throat. Only one man would dare attack her. Only one…

"Ah, so my little wife has decided to become a whore."

She chose her words carefully, "I never was, nor will I ever be, a whore, Matthew."

Her blood was boiling from both anger and fear as he leaned next to her ear and whispered, "You will always be MY whore." Her throat felt dry as she tried to swallow. The move was short lived as the pain began. He dug the knife in a little, causing a trickle of blood to run down her neck. "I think I should be introduced to your new little conquest. Your new little romp… Whore, why don't you scream for him." Deep within she knew it was not a suggestion, but a demand. Years of his abuse came rushing back to her. The memories as vivid as the day each offense occurred. This time though, anger came with the memories, not just fear. — an anger so deep it shook her to the core. Slamming her mouth shut, jarring her teeth, she refused to speak.

"Oh, you're just now deciding to clam up. Tsk, tsk, tsk, and last night you were so verbal with all the moaning." He leaned down and bit the other side of her neck. Her knees threatened to buckle from the mix of fear and anger churning in her stomach as he sucked lightly on her soft flesh, the same spot Alec had marked mere hours before. Matthew was definitely pissed. There was no escaping it, he was going to kill her. "You'll moan like that for me, my little whore."

Amy's face contorted, her rage showed. A whispered, "Never," in defiance escaped between her clenched teeth. He just smirked and tightened his fist in her hair. "I knew he was special when I saw you two together." He took the knife and cut a line from the top of the shirt to the swell of her breasts. "You know, I planned to kill you while you were hanging from the rope. I had a rifle with you in the sights." Her eyes widened. "I came up with a new plan once I saw him though. I knew he wouldn't leave you once he caught your scent." He took in an eyeful of the love marks Alec had left on her skin.

"Tsk. Tsk. This is my property. I can't have another man marking my property." He pressed the blade against her chest, "let's just see what you're lover thinks when he sees your blood." He drug the blade from below her hyoid down to her sternum and frowned when she refused to give him a response to the blood he had drawn. "Hold out your arms," he commanded. Shakily she did. If he killed her before Alec found them then Alec would still be safe.

Matthew smiled gleefully. "Let's see you withstand

this." He brought the blade down into her arm and drug up her forearm to the side of her elbow. "Put your arms down," and she did. No blood came for a few seconds as she tried to ignore the pain, then the dam broke though and the blood gushed. The wound was a centimeter deep and a foot long.

Amy heard the doorknob turn and she looked up in fear. "Amy, lass, Mum sent me to fetch ye for breakfast…" The voice trailed off as Tavish saw in the room. He took in Amy's pain and fear filled eyes. "Lass…" She silently watched as his eyes grew cold with anger. Then his eyes focused on her body. She knew he saw the blood dripping down her chest and arms. His voice took on a frosty tinge, "Lad, let her go now."

Matthew grinned wildly and pressed the blade harder to her throat, drawing another small stream of blood. "Is this him, whore?"

Amy whispered, "No."

He jerked her head back harder causing the blade to once again knick her throat, "No, what?"

"No, my loving husband," Amy closed her eyes as she said it. She hated saying that and he knew it. Bile rose in her throat with the words. He always made her call him a loving husband when he was beating her. It made him feel powerful.

Tavish stepped fully into the room. "Lad, touch her again and I'll let my brother kill ye."

"Like this?" Matthew pulled her head back and descended on her mouth with bruising force. The brutal kiss was not enough for him though. He bit her lip, drawing a tiny bit of blood.

She went limp and as soon as she felt Matthew's grip loosen just a bit, she flew into action. She brought her right knee up and brought the heel of her foot crashing down on his right foot. She grabbed the hand that held the knife with one hand and elbowed him with the other arm. Then she spun on her left foot and punched him as hard as she could in the throat before turning to run. Unfortunately, she didn't get very far as Matthew still had a firm grip on her hair. At the top of her lungs she screamed, "Alec!"

Matthew pulled her back to him and dropped the knife. Tavish ran forward to try to get to him, but Matthew had pulled out a gun. He pointed it at Tavish. "Don't move another step," he said in a deadly tone. Tavish held up his hands as Alec came running in the room with a towel around his waist. "So there is the bastard you've been screwing behind my back."

Amy felt the fear disappear at the sight of Alec. A surge of anger took its place. Her words came out as a scream, "I'm not screwing anybody behind your back!"

Matthew put the gun to her temple. "Shut up and do what you're told. You'd think you'd remember the punishment for cheating on me, but apparently the time apart has caused you to forget."

Her eyes narrowed, "I've never cheated on you, Matthew."

"Oh, yeah, what about Bahrain?"

"I didn't cheat on you then and I'm not cheating on you now!" She cast Alec a sad look.

Matthew snorted. "So who did you screw then?"

"I didn't screw anybody, jerk!"

He tapped the gun to the side of her head. "Don't forget I have the gun…Why don't you tell your little lover here about the tanker. I think it'd be good for him to know what he just slept with," Matthew declared.

Amy lowered her eyes to the ground and refused to speak. An evil smile passed over Matthew's face as he turned and brought up his knee. At the same time he pushed her head forward towards the ground, so that his knee connected with her stomach. Her knees buckled as the air fled from her lungs, but she did not fall to the ground. She refused to kneel at his feet. "Tell them." She shook her head and he sighed. "Fine." He motioned for Tavish and Alec to step to the far corner of the room.

Alec gave him an evil glare, his hands fisted at his sides. "Ye willna live much longer."

Matthew laughed, a sadistic sound that grated on Amy's ears. "Oh, I think I will. See this pretty gem right here has a habit of making people want her, you fell for it after all, and I know a lot of men that would pay to get a shot at her for a night. Some even want to find out just what she knows…"

Her eyes went wide in fear and she sought Alec out, silently begging him to save her. "We're going to leave without anybody getting in our way or else I'm going to shoot her in the head. Trust me, there's no coming back from a two inch hole in your temple." He leaned forward and whispered in Amy's ear, "that's what happened to Jer. My boy failed me. All because of you."

Amy gave a slight nod at Alec and Alec ushered Tavish over to the other side of the room. While they never had their backs turned, they focused on their prey. That is what Matthew was to them, prey. They would save her, she just had to have faith. However, as Matthew started dragging Amy to the door leading into the room, that faith was hard to keep. He kept both the guys and the door in sight at all times. "Don't worry, we're going to have some fun," he sneered at her.

Matthew's eyes were slightly glazed and Amy knew he had taken some drugs. Guessing he was on cocaine again, as that was his drug of choice, but Amy was not sure. People some times changed. Maybe in their time apart he had branched out in to other things.

He continued to drag her out the door and then out the front door with Rory, Ian, Sheena, and Alan staring in anger. "If I see or hear anything unusual I will kill her just for spite." They stood back as he shut the door.

Amy glanced at the door as he slammed it shut and felt all of her hope at a new life, one without Matthew Killigan, vanish into thin air. A solitary tear rolled down her left cheek as Matthew jerked her towards the woods. The sound of her heart breaking was one she would never forget. It seemed so loud, yet, no one else heard. "You won't get away with this," she whispered.

He tightened his grip on her hair. "Oh really, you think so?" There was a sadistic smile on his face. "I don't need to get away with it. I just need to make sure he won't have you." The fear that he would kill her rather than let her go, which had taken root in her stomach after he had first hurt her so many years ago and had simmered since, began to spread like wildfire throughout her entire body. She tripped over a small log on the ground as they entered the woods. "You are going to wish you never looked at another man when I'm through with you."

CHAPTER 24

ALEC, TAVISH, RORY, AND IAN watched through the window as Matthew drug Amy across the grass. No one knew how he had made it past Riley and Rocky, but he had. Both dogs were silent… It was time to put a stop to his reign of terror. As Matthew entered the woods with Amy, Alan placed his hand upon Alec's shoulder. Alan frowned, the gravity of the situation hit home in more ways than one. There would be no more loss in this family. One child had been enough. "Boys, if it's between her and that bloody tosser make sure ye pick her. I don't want my sons killin', but that good for nothing deserves a world of hurt."

Alec's eyes glowed, his fists were clenched, and he exuded anger. "Dinnae worry, Da'. I promise he will feel it…" Alan knew what his son had promised Amy. Whether it had been spoken or not did not matter. He had promised it. A MacDaniel always kept his promises. His son was going to keep his promise to Amy if it killed him. Nobody was going to hurt her ever again. Alan knew that his sons could always be counted on to protect a woman. After all, he had raised them and he had raised them right, even the son that he had lost.

Sheena still believed he lived because no body had been found, but in war sometimes no body was ever found. He dreaded the day they did find one. He dreaded the day the light fled from her eyes. For now, they could save Amy. In doing so they could also save Alec. They saw Amy cast one lingering glance at the Inn before the two disappeared from view. "Now!"

Sheena and Alan watched as their four boys ran out of the Inn after Amy. "Alan, think they remember what their grandda' taught them?"

Alan laughed. "I doubt they ever forgot."

His words brought a smile to her face. "Yer right, our boys will always remember how to be wankers."

They might, but they were also his children. He had raised them to protect, but offer clemency. Unfortunately, there came a time when it was past offering clemency... "Wife of mine, call the doctor an' get him on his way. I will get some blankets for the puir wee thing from the back and go meet them." She could not know what he was really doing. It was time to put a stop to that man, time to put a stop to his reign of terror. His sons might let him live and he would come again. It might be years, but he would come again. He would never accept it. Alan knew this because he had seen his type many years ago. Never would he forget the look in that man's eyes... Steeling himself to do what needed to be done, he began the long walk down the hall. There was one room in the house that was never opened. In fact, he himself held the only key. As he slipped it from his pocket he fought the tears that threatened to overwhelm him. A parent should never outlive a child. Never.

CHAPTER 25

AMY BIT HER LIP TO keep from crying out as stepped on a sharp rock. It was better to make no sound. Maybe he would not hurt her if she was quiet. Alec needed as much time as she could give him. He would come for her, she just had to remember that. The pain continued as he drug her further through the woods. She was pretty sure her feet were dirty and bleeding as Matthew had not exactly given her time to put on her shoes.

Wait. There were numerous ways she could stall him. Why was she going quietly? *Still in the train of thought of being quiet are we?* This was the end. He had promised to kill her after all. Why be quiet for it? Why make it easy for him? Alec would come. He would save her again, she just had to stall Matthew long enough for Alec to find them. "Why are you doing this? Why can't you just accept that you screwed up and leave me alone?"

He stopped abruptly and turned her to face him. Rage reflected back at her through his face. In all the times he had hurt her he had never once looked angry. He had always looked resigned, like he thought he was doing it for her benefit. This was different. He was pissed. *Yep, definitely going to die today. At least it'll be over. Finally free from him*, she thought.

He brought the gun up underneath her chin. "You think that's what's going on here?" He laughed. "You cheated on me and you think I screwed up! You certainly are a precocious bitch."

Amy's eyes narrowed. Bravely she pushed the gun to the side, "I didn't cheat on you, jerk!"

Smack! Her head whipped to the side from the force of his slap. "Yes you did."

She turned back to him, blood trickling from her nose. "No, I didn't. You were destroying the lives of children! You were using children as mules to take drugs across the border for you! You were ruining their lives and getting them killed! Children that couldn't protect themselves! I had to do something. I couldn't just let you hurt them! I didn't have a choice!"

His face turned deadly. "You didn't have a choice? You went to the DEA and ratted me out! You cost me my job and got me in trouble with the Cartel. Do you even have a clue what I had to do to survive that?"

"I know what you did," she hissed. "You murdered a DEA Agent!"

"I don't have to justify what I did to you. You are my wife…"

"Was!"

"What?"

She smirked in triumph, it was time. Finally! After so long, it was time… "Ever heard of something called an annulment?" His eyes narrowed. Obviously he had no idea that he had lost her so long ago. Growing bolder she continued, "A marriage isn't legally binding if one party, me, doesn't sign the wedding certificate. The funny thing is that you can sure get a divorce or an annulment without two signatures. They grant annulments if the wedding certificate isn't valid."

He put the gun back underneath her chin. "Doesn't matter," he shrugged, "Nobody will want you when I'm done. I'll make sure of it." He then let go of her and tore the shirt the rest of the way down. "Take it off," he commanded as he licked his lips.

She heard a bird off to her left and heard an answering response on her right. She smiled, Alec was coming for her. She had only known him for a few short days, but after the episode at the Falls, she knew he would keep his promise. Her heart told her so. It told her in the way that it beat faster around him or when she thought of him. It told her in the way it stopped when she thought Matthew was going to kill him. It even told her so in the way that it broke at the thought of never seeing him again.

Alec would protect her, when no one else had. He would save her, when no one else, save Finn, had ever tried. The difference was that he would succeed. Her Highlander was coming for her. Her family would have loved him. They were gone though. Now that she thought about it, she realized that her parents had died not long after she met Matthew. Had he had something to do with that as well? She wouldn't put it past the bastard.

"Fine, Matthew," she sneered, "take it!" She pulled the shirt off and threw it at him. "It's all yours. What else do you want? Do you want the boxers too?" She pushed them down and stepped out of them. "There, they're all yours too!" She stood their naked as the day she was born, defying him, her head held high.

His face went red. Knowing what was coming did not make it any easier to take when he punched her. The force of it sent her to the ground. She wiped blood from her lip before standing up again, never would she bow or kneel at his feet. Never again. She was shaking from fear as she steeled herself for another punch and she was not disappointed. This time he jerked her up from the ground. "We don't have time for this." He pushed her forward, laughing as she stumbled, and walked behind her. Amy hoped she had given Alec enough time to get in front of them, but as she heard the rush of water she was not so sure.

They had walked two miles, Amy guessed, when they stepped out from behind some trees and she saw it. They were standing at the top of the Falls of Mesach. The roar of the water was now all around her. This was it. This was the end. Matthew leaned forward, his breath hot on her ear. "If I can't have you neither can he." He forced her to walk to the edge, the suspension bridge off in the distance. She looked towards the spot where she had almost fallen to her death. Alec had been the one to save her then and he would be the one to save her now. He had to be.

"You know, Ames, if you hadn't been such a bitch this wouldn't have happened. We could still be happy living in our little townhouse in San Diego. Maybe even have a couple of kids by now."

Ignoring the pain in her upper arm, held tightly in his grasp, she whipped around to face him. "You're fucking delusional!"

"That may be, but you can't ignore it."

He grinned. The bastard actually grinned. The anger simmering in her blood all these years began to boil. She wrentched her arm from his ironlike clasp and hopped away from him. "You're just an asshole. You can't get me in bed, so you have to force me. I wonder why that is? Could it be that you're just really bad in bed?" She knew she had pushed him over the edge with that remark and quickly began murmuring the Lord's Prayer as he stalked towards her.

He grabbed her by the throat and lifted her up. "I'm done playing games with you." He threw her down and she landed hard on her side. He kicked her with his boot and forced her on her back. A sharp rock bit into her back as he sat on her. He reached up and pushed a lock of hair behind her ear in an almost loving gesture. She knew the truth — the awful truth. There was nothing loving about anything he did. There never had been.

"Why don't we let you find out, after all, it has been a while." He reached to unzip his jeans with one hand while the other pointed the gun at Amy. It was in that moment, of what should have been desperation, that a feeling of complete and total calm stole over her. It was the same feeling the ocean always gave her, even after it rescued her from her attackers. Floating along, the waves had protected her. They had ensconced her in a cocoon of safety and that feeling once again swept over her.

A twig gave a slight crack off to the side. Alec had come for her. She smirked at the knowledge of what was to come. Matthew misinterpreted the reason. "Oh, so you do remember," he whispered.

She shook her head. "No, just realized how cracked out you really are." A sharp whistle sounded from a few feet away and she looked behind Matthew, causing him to turn his head to see what she was looking at. Her smirk grew into a shit eating grin. It was time. It was finally time for her to return the favor. As he turned back to her, she punched him as hard as she could right in the nose. She had been waiting years to do that. As he fell backwards from the force of it he was jerked off of her by Alec and tossed in Rory's direction. Rory brought up his leg as if he was going to do a front snap kick, but he instead brought his foot quickly down, at an angle, onto Matthew's knee cap. Amy heard a sickening crunch and almost felt bad for him. Almost. Matthew would never walk right again.

Tavish was right beside Rory and punched Matthew with a jab to the right eye as Ian helped her up. They had all come for her. Quiet as thieves in the night, they had stolen upon them to save her.

Ian, bless his heart, was being extremely careful to keep his eyes on her face as she stood. "Lass, are ye alright?" She nodded and he slipped his maroon t-shirt over his head. Handing it to her, he whispered, "Put this on." There was no argument raised as she did what he told her to. Words had failed her. Here these men were, protecting her, without regard to their personal safety. They all had come for her. After years of being abandoned and neglected, they all had come for her. Tears threatened at the corner of her eyes. The family she had lost had, in some small way, been returned to her.

Her eyes were intently honed on Alec as he grabbed Matthew's wrist. The SNAP resounded off the canyon walls. Matthew's arm was at a funny angle. Alec had snapped his arm at the elbow. Relief flooded her knowing he would never touch her again. Ian tried to turn her so she did not see it, but she refused. The MacDaniel brothers were like a band of angry wolves hell bent on getting revenge as they descended on Matthew Killigan, the idiot who had dared to hurt a member of their pack, without mercy. This caused Amy to smile brightly. After a lifetime of pain someone was finally standing up for her, and winning. They were getting revenge for her, revenge for Finn, revenge for the Deputy, revenge for the DEA Agent, possibly even revenge for her parents.

When Rory and Tavish had decided enough blood had been drawn from Matthew Killigan they glanced at Amy, whose eyes were fastened on Alec, who was still trying to pummel Matthew's body into a bloody pulp. Neither made a move to stop him. They were letting her decide when enough was enough. After all, she was the one that had suffered at the bastard's hands. "Alec," she whispered as she stepped forward. Slowly reaching out a shaking hand, she placed her hand on his arm to stop him from causing further harm. It was so cold. The wind was coming off the falls along with a fine mist. "Alec, I'm tired and I think the blood loss is getting to me. Will you please take me home?"

Alec stopped in mid punch the moment her hand had touched his arm. He turned and looked at her. She knew that her eyes shone with love for him and it made her proud — proud that she could feel such a feeling again. Her mouth quirked in a small smile.

"Amy…," at saying her name the anger in him seemed to fade away. Releasing a deep breath, he turned away from Matthew and towards her. She shivered as he ran a finger along her cheek bone. "Will ye forgive me for letting him hurt you?"

"That depends," stepping forward and putting his hands on her waist she whispered, "on how you plan on making it up to me." She looked up at him through her eyelashes, unsure of whether he understood her meaning. Turning away from Matthew her life was finally her own again. So many years now, and freedom was finally within her grasp. She simply had to reach out and grab a new life with both hands. That new life would include Alec if he would let it.

CHAPTER 26

A S ALEC PICKED HER UP to carry her home she tried to bury herself in his chest. Soaking in the smell of him, the warmth he gave off. His warmth was not just body heat, it was love, protection, safety, and generosity — everything that she had never had before. How on Earth had she not known what she was missing? All those years of being alone, fearing for her life, and she had not realized what she could have sought.

"This isn't over!" Her head whipped up as Alec turned around to face Matthew. Blood poured from his nose and mouth, several teeth were missing courtesy of the Mac-Daniel brothers. His bones crunched as he attempted to stand, a gun in his hand. "If I can't have you then no one can."

Crack!

Amy jumped in Alec's arms clutching to him. "No! Not again!" Searching for a wound, as he gently sat her on the ground, sobs tore from her throat. Where was the blood? A scream tore through the air! Glancing up at Alec's face she saw his gaze riveted to where Matthew stood. Turning she prepared to charge Matthew, tear him limb from limb, rip out his heart and feed it to him.

Only... he stood there with his hands over his stomach. Blood seeped through his fingers.

He looked at her with a lost look, "Amy, I did love you." Placing his arms out with his palms up to the sky he closed his eyes. Stepping one step backwards he grinned, "You'll always remember this." He jumped back and screamed, a primordial scream full of hatred and anger.

He no longer stood at the edge. He was gone. He had jumped over the side towards the craggy rocks below. Had he really jumped or was she imagining it? Looking at Alec to confirm it she noticed that he was looking towards the woods where the bullet came from.

A man came out of the woods, with a rifle in his hands. It was Alan. Was the shot...? Had the shot come from Alan? Was Matthew dead? She left Alec's side. Cautiously stepping closer to the edge, she had to know, she just had to know. Holding her breath she peered over the side. Matthew was gone. He was truly gone. Was it real? Turning back she saw Alan approach his sons, his head down, as if in shame.

"Never thought I would use this. Danny's..."

Rory placed a hand on his father's shoulder. "Da, Danny would be proud. He left it for protection. Tis the perfect time to use it." Alan looked up to his sons. "Yer mother doesna know. She cannae know. Ever."

Amy watched helplessly. He had just used his dead son's rifle to kill Matthew, to save her. She did the only thing she could. Ignoring both the pain in her body and the lightheadedness from blood loss, she cautiously stepped forward. This she could do, this family that loved each other with everything they had. Even if they fought, they still bound together.

Gently, she took the rifle from him. It was heavier than she remembered rifles being. Sadness filled her. They had given so much for her. She gave it to Rory. The rifle had saved them, but with that it brought so much pain. How would they ever be whole again? "Alan, thank you. From the bottom of my heart, thank you." She hugged him. "I can never repay what you and your sons have done for me. I am truly sorry that I have brought such pain to your family."

Alan choked back a sob, "Lass, ye never apologize for this again. Twas a just thing to do. Rory's right. Danny left the rifle for protection. He always wanted his family to be kept safe. Even if he could not be here to do the job his self. I am proud of all my sons. All of them. Whether tis but a memory in my heart or he stands proud in front of me." He took a deep breath, seemingly to steady himself. "Time to go home. Rory, hide the gun in the jeep. I will get it later to put it back where it was, where Danny left it."

Alec wrapped his arms around her from behind as Alan removed the blanket from over his shoulder. "Son, wrap her well. The doctor should be at the Inn momentarily to stitch her wounds. Yer mum fetched him for her. Then we shall call the magistrate."

The scream... It would never leave her. Never for as long as she lived would she forget that sound, shrill and keening as he fell below. Should she be upset at his death? Or should she be relieved that he would never harm her again? That last thought made her feel insignificant, made her feel as if she deserved to remember his scream for all eternity, as if she deserved to have it haunt her every waking and sleeping moment. Would Alec forgive her for thinking such?

She buried herself further into his comforting arms. The way they were wrapped around her made her feel loved. His warmth bled through the maroon shirt as he carefully picked her up. At the same time he was picking up the broken pieces of her soul. He had come for her. Matthew had tried to kill her, but Alec had saved her. He had once again kept his word, proving that he was truthful. With each step he took she felt free, freer than she had in so long. Matthew was dead. Alec was carrying her away from the Falls. With each step he held her closer to his chest, cradling her to him, whispering kind words to her. His father and brothers flanked them, protecting her. Not once in her life had she ever been so safe.

"Sweet, lass. Och, sweet, sweet, lass. I am so sorry fer yer pain."

CHAPTER 27

FORTY-ONE STITCHES, THAT'S WHAT IT took to close her wounds, Alec thought, and he knew because he had counted. He had counted every single one. He frowned as he watched the doctor close off the last one. It was his fault. She was injured while in his care. He should have been more cautious, more prepared. If he had, this wouldn't have happened. She wouldn't have needed forty-one stitches...

Looking up, he caught sight of the omnipotent smirk on her face. That smirk drew him like a moth to a flame, made him wonder what in the world was on her mind. What could she know that he did not? She seemed happy despite everything that had happened. How could that be possible? Who knew if the people behind Matthew Killigan's actions knew where she was. What if they were planning on coming for her too? Or had the deceased man really acted alone? It wasn't safe for her with him. Alec obviously couldn't protect anyone. He couldn't protect Morvena. He couldn't protect Amy.

The doctor sighed, interrupting Alec's thoughts. "That should do it. Lass, ye need to stay away from these Mac-Daniels because I'm not addin' another stitch." The small smile on his face said he was joking with her. He would patch her as much as she needed. Alec knew this because the doctor had patched him enough as a child, always joking that it would be the last time.

"Don't worry, I'm safe now," Amy beamed, her face picture perfect innocence and naivety.

Alec felt as if a fist had closed over his heart; squeezing and mashing until it was no longer beating for anything other than her. She was so beautiful, yet she truly had no idea. *Maybe I should tell her*, he thought as he reached up and pushed one of her many curls behind her ear, causing her smile to grow. Words, however, refused to come. Amy slipped her hand into his and stood up from the old wooden chair. "So am I all good, Doc?"

"Aye, yer all good, but make sure you keep them dry for twenty-four hours. I made sure they were small and tight, so scarrin' should be minimal," the doctor said as he put his things back in his bag. "Come by my office immediately if they look infected. Ye know what to look for?" Amy nodded as the doctor turned a look fit to kill on Alec. "Lad, if she causes ye any trouble tie her down to the bed."

Alec's eyes went wide like a deer caught in headlights as images filtered through his mind — dirty, interesting, and thought provoking images of positions that he would love to try with her. Lusty thoughts vanished as Amy smiled at him. So many stitches, yet she still smiled.

"Thanks, doc. I think Alec will make sure there's not any more added any time soon though."

Such trust she had in him... Where did it come from? She had almost died, how could she trust him? He almost lost her. Maybe she was safer back in the states now that the bastard was dead, where she had a life.

"See that he does, lass. See that he does."

He would alright. He would make sure that she never needed another stitch again, by sending her home. Yes, she would be safer there, where no more harm could come to her. If he could not protect her in his family home then there was nowhere that he could protect her. To save her he needed to let her go back to where she would be safe. It was the only way he could let her go. Leaning down he kissed her lightly on her forehead. "Yer safe now, lass. No more harm shall come to ye." Then he walked out.

A pain blossomed in his chest. It was unfair finding someone to love after all of these years, after all that he had lost. After closing himself off to everything other than his family... and then letting them go. It was unfair, cruel, evil. There were many other words he would prefer to use instead, many of them four letters long.

Leaning against the wall, he wondered if Morvena would despise him for falling in love again. Perhaps he had not been in love with her at all. Why would it be so easy to fall in love with Amy if he had ever loved Morvena? Maybe it was the fact that Amy needed him more than Morvena ever had. Maybe it was the fact that Morvena never loved him. He still needed to do right by her. He had married her, so the cross was his to bear. Would she be angry with him? He was after all courting a married lass. True, her husband was dead now. His own father had made sure of that. Mourning takes time though. He knew that better than most. Grief is a strong beast, making someone do things that they ordinarily would never do. If she stayed with him would she do it just because of grief? Or would she love him? Could she love him?

Morvena's image drifted into his mind, of the day they met. He had been enamored with her, but she hadn't been interested at first. Then he joined the Yard, excelling at the Specialist Operations area where he went up against organized crime in the bowels of the city. London had been his home. Now... it was just full of bad memories. Memories of Morvena lying dead, blood pooling around her.

A slow, deep breath served to strengthen his resolve. *The lass needs time to mourn, in her own way.* It was time to send her home, even if all he wanted was her by his side, for eternity.

He had to do something. He had to prove he was worthy of her. Right now, he wasn't worthy of anyone. He was still broken and he was tainted. His soul still ached. He would re-join the Yard. He would do his damnedest to make sure no one else suffered as Amy had. He would try to protect as many as he could. Maybe that would make him worthy of her. He wanted to be worthy of her, but if he couldn't be then he would help as many as he could.

CHAPTER 28

AS AMY LOOKED AT THE entrance to the airport she felt disheartened. Alec didn't want her. Her shoulders slumped. Alec hadn't wanted her when she had been willing to put aside her past, all the trauma she had endured, and hand him her heart. Hell, it had been wrapped up with a pretty bow even, then he handed it back to her — a precious gift and he had rejected it. The question was not why. She knew why. The question was how he thought it was ok to do so. That was the question.

Slowly turning back, she looked at Rory who held both her bag and Rocky's leash, the same bag the Sheriff's deputy had packed for her in her mad rush to flee the country. Now it almost seemed stupid. She had won though. Her plan might not have worked, but Alec had still saved her. His family had still saved her, someone they did not even know. They put their lives on the line against a bastard all because Alec asked them to — just like Finn had. They only difference is that Finn had given up his life for her. Alec and his family were still alive. Maybe one day she would have a family like that again. Maybe she would meet someone that wanted her, someone willing to save her because they loved her. For now it was time to say goodbye, time to move on. If Alec did not want her, then she would not stay.

"Well, Rory, it was nice to meet you. Thank you for everything that you and your family have done for me. You have no idea how much it means to me. I'll honestly never forget it or you guys."

Shifting from foot to foot, Rory used his free hand to push his hair back from his face. In the short time that she had known him, Amy had come to recognize it as a nervous habit. "Aye, lass. Ye have won my heart."

Tears began to well up in her eyes. Clearing her throat she whispered, "But not Alec's apparently."

He sighed deeply and cast his eyes downward. "Lass, tis much that ye dinnae know."

"All that's needed to know is that he packed my clothes for me within minutes of the last stitch being put in place." He even brought it down to her and waited while she put on warm clothes. "I fell in love with him. He only wanted me gone…" That hurt a lot more than she was willing to admit.

"Lass…"

No, she did not want to hear his excuses. It was not up to him to make her feel better. They had already done so much for her. "Don't start. I'm headed home. Everything's fine. He saved me and I'll never forget that. It was just natural that he no longer wanted me. It's ok. I'm a grown up. I can handle it. Please tell your family that I said thank you for everything. I sincerely mean that too."

As she turned away from him he grabbed her arm. Old reflexes kicked in causing her to flinch. "Lass, Alec was wed to a lass that dinnae love him. She died from a gunshot just before she was to be givin' birth to the bairn the sod believed twas his. Alec was investigatin' a crime with the Yard. He thought her safe, but was gone fer more than she liked. Her betrayal is what cost her life. The killer would not have found her if she had nae been at her lover's home.

"Alec tis a good man. Even if he blames himself for Morvena's follies. Me brother is a wee bit off when it comes to love. He seems to be out of practice at that game. The sod just needs time. Time to realize what is right in front of him."

Grabbing her bag and Rocky's leash she took a deep breath. Alec should have told her that he lost the woman he was married to. Alec should have been the one to tell her that his wife had been killed, especially after everything he had learned about her. At the airport she had asked who Morvena was and he had lied to her. Was that a lack of trust? Or had he been afraid to tell her because of the situation?

Everything had moved so quickly. Was she really ready to trust her heart with someone that she did not know that much about? Was she really ready to put her faith in a man that had lied to her, no matter the motives?

Her shoulders slumped. Yes. The answer was definitely yes. He meant more to her than Matthew ever could have. It would not matter if he had been the best husband in the entire world, he still would never have lived up to love she felt for Alec.

"Love isn't a game. It's serious business. The most serious business of all." Life was the game. It had to be lived well and without regrets. If she left without leaving Alec an inkling of how she felt, she would regret it for the rest of her life.

"If he changes his mind, he knows where to find me. I've talked with Dylan and I go back to work tomorrow morning. I need to get a life. It's been too long since I lived. If Alec chooses to come for me, it won't be so easy for him. He's going to have to prove himself." He would too. Of that she had no doubt. As strange as it was she loved him, and trusted him, now he just needed to show that he felt the same.

"Give the wanker hell." His words brought a grin to her face.

"I assure you that I plan to. He won't know what hit him if he ever decides that he wants to come for me." She truly believed that he would come for her, Amy just hoped that he would finally realize just how much she needed him, and come for her sooner rather than later.

"Alec will come for ye. I bet me life upon it."

CHAPTER 29

ALEC LOOKED UP AS A glass of whiskey was placed in front of him. "Da?"

"Son, ye be my pride, but ye have a long way to go in learnin' about love." Pulling the chair back from the table, the soft scrape on the floor made Alec feel as if he was facing the gallows. Only the gallows would have been a quicker death. "Son, I know ye love the lass. Ye give her the same look I gave yer mum when we were wee things, fresh in love… Why send her away?"

As he sat down he cast Alec a look of confusion mixed with understanding. His da had been there once before, after all. Alec knew he was the one man that would understand, understand why he had to send her away, even if it was as clear as muddy water.

"Amy, such a special lass. Sweet as the heather, fresh as the sky on a clear day… Da, I love her. God, tis true, I love her." Raising the glass to his lips he tossed the contents back, reveling in the sweet burn of the whiskey as it made it's way down his throat. "Love is not the issue though. The lass needs time to mourn her husband. I cannae keep Amy safe." The words tasted sour on his tongue, like a bucket full of lemons mixed with a week's worth of trash had invaded his mouth.

"Alec, ye truly are not the son I raised. The son I raised would have talked to his love before…" His father stopped and took a deep calming breath. "That twas not the lass' husband. Amy Killigan was a free one." Pulling a piece of paper from his pocket he sat it on the table. "Yer a bloody fool, Alec. A right bloody fool." He pushed the paper forward.

Picking it up Alec's eyes focused on the large printed words at the top of the page. "Dissolution of Marriage…" Scanning further down his eyes began to water and his throat began to close up. His voice cracked as he whispered, "She was free…" And had been for years, according to the paper. Scanning down the page his stomach flipped. According to the paper Amy was not only free, but she had sought the divorce while being a star witness in the trial against her husband, a witness against him for his crimes of drug running. Amy had survived so much. Alec knew she was strong, but he didn't realize just how strong she was. To fight against the man you married, to right a wrong, then be all alone and tortured by that same man for trying to do what was right… She deserved more than what Alec had given her. She deserved better from him.

Pushing the chair back, Alan stood and leaned over the table. As he placed both palms on the table he shook his head, "Bloody fool, Alec. Yer a bloody fool." Standing fully upright he crossed his arms over his chest. "Ye made a right mess of things. Aye, a right mess. Ye have to decide how to make things right with the lass. Dinnae wait too long, Alec. Love tis in her heart, but fer how long?"

Had he really made a mess of everything?

Alan frowned at him, the lines in his face etched in

concern. "Something ye ferget, Alec, if the tosser worked fer men worse than him… yer lass is unprotected."

As Alec watched his father walk away he wondered for how long indeed. Would she forgive him? Would she accept him? Would she still love him? What if she was unable to forgive him no matter how hard or how long he begged? His stomach clenched. What if her ex had told the men he worked for that she was a threat to them? What if Alec had lost her by sending her home?

Deciding it was time to go after her he folded up the paper neatly. It would not do to leave it somewhere that it was not safe. He would need it if she was accepting of him, and his apology. First, he had to get to her.

"Alec," he looked up to see Rory standing there in the doorway. His brother casually leaned against the wood, his arms crossed over his chest. "Yer lass is on the plane. Should land in North Carolina about the time ye get on the next flight." Rory held up a ticket. "Not sure ye need to take anything. Might as well leave yer pride here before the lass squashes it like a bug."

Rory's words brought a grin to his face. It was not too late it seemed. "Ye think she will 'ave me?"

"Och, such a fool ye are." He stepped forward and tossed the ticket onto the table. "Why the lass chose ye when she could 'ave me…"

Alec stood up quickly, knocking the chair back. "Ye willna lay a hand on my lass!"

"Yer the one that let her go. Aye, ye did indeed. Now tis time for ye to decide what to do 'bout it."

He was right. "Aye, tis time indeed." Scooping up the ticket he knew his decision had been made the very first moment he had met Amy Killigan. An angel had fallen from the sky and landed… on him. That should have been the clue. If Morvena had made it to Heaven she had sent him his true love, the one woman that was his match in every way. As he raced out of the Inn, he decided that he would forgive everything Morvena had done to him if she was the one responsible for such a gift.

CHAPTER 30

A LEC SLOWLY OPENED THE DOOR to the small outdoors store. As long as she did not throw a book at him when he first walked in, then he could hope that they would work it out. That maybe, just maybe she would forgive him in time. Admitting you were a bloody tosser was hard work. Admitting that you were one because you were in love, well, that was easy and totally acceptable. In this case, groveling was acceptable as well.

When nothing came flying in his direction he took a hesitant step inside. "You're safe. She's in the back." He looked for the voice and found it belonged to a man in a Hawaiian shirt. "Ames doesn't think you would dare show your face here just yet. Said something about you being a crazy Scot that wouldn't know love if it punched you in the face. The kid may have also mentioned something about punching you when she saw you, so watch out for her right cross. It's downright painful." He rubbed his jaw as if she had recently punched him. "She also said you saved her life and did something that she honestly never thought anyone would do for her… By the way, I'm Dylan, her boss."

"Nice to meet ye, Dylan."

"Likewise, but you have your work cut out for you. Ha! I definitely don't envy you one bit. Shouldn't be too hard if you find the right way though. You're the only man she's ever spoken of. Unfortunately, it looks like there might be a bit of an intervention needed. You taking her back to Scotland?"

"If she will allow it."

He nodded lost in thought. "Let me get her from the back. I think it's time I pushed the chick out of the nest." Turning to the door off to his right he walked through it. "Ames, come here for a sec!" He hollered the words, making Alec jump.

A few seconds later Alec heard her. "You're firing me?"

"Yep, time you stepped out and learned to fly. Life's passing you by, go grab it with both hands and hold on for the ride."

"I tried that and it didn't work out."

"It did, you just don't know it yet. By the way, you've got a visitor out front. He's tall, Scottish, and is waiting for you to throw something at him."

In the ensuing silence Alec worried that she was trying to find the biggest thing within her reach to throw at him. When she appeared in the doorframe empty handed, he released the breath he had been holding.

He threw his hands up to signal surrender. "Lass, please. Just hear me out."

"No! I'm done listening to people. Let me make it clear for you. Sod off! You understood that one, right?"

With a small smile he stepped forward. "Lass, I'm Scottish. Not British."

"You're an ass is what you are!"

"Aye, that bit is true." Reaching out he took her hand. "Aye, that bit is true indeed."

"I don't know if I can ever forgive you."

"I dinnae expect ye to forgive me."

"Good!"

He watched her try to pull away lightly. Her eyes cut up towards his. "Lass, my mistake twas in lovin' ye." She jerked her hand from his and spun around. Her shoulders were hunched up as she grabbed her backpack from the countertop. "Amy, I loved ye too much. I canna protect ye though, so I sent ye away for protection. I sent ye away, so ye'd be safe."

She spun around, her face was bright red and tears ran down her cheeks. The golden flakes within her eyes shone brightly as if reflecting the fire of her anger back at him. If looks could kill he would be struck dead, fried up, and served for dinner. "Safe from who!?! Matthew's dead, finally! After all these years he's dead…"

"Safe from me. Morvena… she died because of me. She dinnae love me. Aye, I knew, but I tried to make her love me. Morvena was shot by a man who's boss I was chasin'. A man that hopefully will spend the rest of his years in prison. Meanwhile, two lovers were broken by my actions. I dinnae want the same fate for ye. My heart breaks at yer pain, Amy. My soul cries for yers. My soul burns for ye, Amy. A fiery hot longin' strikes to my verra core. I dinnae go a second without thinkin' of ye, Amy Killigan. I dinnae expect forgiveness. Simply a glimmer of hope that ye still love me."

"Why?" He watched in rapt fascination as she threw her arms up in the air. "You are absolutely hopeless, Alec! Hopeless! Why in the hell I feel this way I don't know! I honestly never thought I would love anyone ever again after what was done to me and then you came along!"

"Correction, then ye fell on me."

"Shut up…" Her face was slightly red as if she was trying not to scream at him. It was quite endearing actually.

"I'm trying to tell you that for some reason, beyond my understanding, I love you and then you go and interrupt…"

He did not let her continue, was not about to. It was what he wanted to hear, what he needed to hear. She still loved him, that was all that mattered. They could work on the rest. He grabbed her and pulled her to him. Swooping in, he kissed her with all the love he felt, all the love he could squeeze into one kiss. In time she would forgive him, but for now he would show her just how much he loved her. He would show her in every action and every word for as long as he lived. After all, she was worth it and so was he.

She broke the kiss and pulled back from him. "Bollocks."

"What?"

"I told you I would use it one day." She grinned at him before throwing her arms around his neck and kissing him again. If that's what she did after using that word, then as far as he was concerned she could use it whenever she wanted. In fact, he hoped she used it quite often.

EPILOGUE

AMY LOOKED UP FROM THE book she was reading in the cushy chair. It still amazed her that she and Alec had found their way to each other. Now he was about to tell his parents their plans. They had talked about it at length. She was amazed that he was including her, making it as much her dream as his. As Alec ushered his family into the room at the Inn, Amy set the book down in her lap. The moment had finally arrived.

"Amy and I have thought a lot about where we want to live and what we want to do."

As Alec came to stand beside her she was filled with pride, pride in the man that she loved and pride in his desire to do the right thing. "I've tried to convince Alec to go back to the Yard, but a friend of his had something different in mind." She smiled and stared at him as she spoke.

"Mac was hurt in the line of duty a while back and has retired. He wants to start up a company with us."

"We want to open a protection agency," Amy clarified.

"What do ye mean?" Alec's father looked worried. His eyes darted back and forth between them.

Amy grabbed Alec's hand and squeezed it, deriving

strength from the motion. "Mac heard about what Alec did for me. There's a lot of people that need help. Some can pay and some can't, but both deserve to be helped. Mac wants to open a company where both are taken care of. Kinda like bodyguards. You know, stop people from getting hurt… Alec and I support the idea and are ready to jump in; however, we wanted to talk to you both first." It was important to her that they support Alec and her decision.

Alec's dad smiled at her, a proud smile. "Tis a fantastic idea!"

Beside her, Alec released the breath he was holding. "Mac knows a few good men. We will need to figure out specifics."

Alec's mother waved his words away, "The specifics will come."

Amy smiled. Not only had Alec saved her and taught her what love really could be, he was now branching out and helping others. She had no idea how she got to be so lucky, but she would take every moment of it with him.

"Where will the company be located?"

The moment of truth, there was no going back once it was out in the open. Taking a deep breath and releasing it slowly, she smiled. "For now, it will be located in London. If it goes well, then we'll branch out."

Alec quickly held up a hand. She had forgotten they might worry about him being inclined to move further away than London. "Nothing will happen right away, but we'll get there. Every plan takes time," Alec explained.

"What will the company be called?"

"We were thinking Unique Kingdom Enterprises or UKE for short."

"Twill be a fine company an' a job to be proud of."

Yes it would. Amy was already proud of Alec for starting it. He was doing it all for her too, but she had asked for him to keep that secret. He wanted her to feel safe and what better way than to start a company that was designed to protect people. In a way it was for him too, so that he never had to leave her again. They could help others together. She just hoped Mac would be up to the task… She hadn't met him yet, but he had lost a lot. Of course, if she could find Alec and come back from the void, then maybe Mac would be ok. Only time would tell…

ABOUT THE AUTHOR

Find Brina on Facebook:
www.facebook.com/brina99cary/?fref=ts